A DAME CALLED DEREK

Book One Diva Diaries
By
Kerrie Noor

CONTENTS

JUST A THOUGHT

Pantomime is the language of laughter,
except where George was concerned

A WEE GLOSSARY

Rabbie Burns (Robert Burns): The ploughman's poet of Scotland who lived fast, died young, and loved a lot. His writings are romantic, philosophical, and political. And, much to the annoyance of some children, often studied in primary school. He is the reason for the proliferation of Burns Suppers all over the world, the rise of the humble Haggis, and the creator of a poem so long that an audience can down two pints and a packet of crisps and even take a comfort break.

Haggis: Although not mentioned in the story, I feel the need to explain. Centuries ago the haggis was the humble food of poor Scottish farmers—spicy leftovers from a butchered sheep minced and stuffed into a sheep's "cleaned and emptied" stomach, and then boiled.

Now, thanks to a love of Rabbie Burns's poetry, including his "O' to a Haggis" poem, the haggis has been elevated to posh nosh in posh restaurants, battered and deep-fried in Indian takeaways, and stuffed into a variety of foods including baked potatoes, chicken breast, and lasagna.

Poosie Nancie: A pub, named after one of Rabbie Burns's lovers: a married woman who ran an inn where some of his poetry was written.

She is often represented at Burns's Supper by a woman carrying in the Haggis on a platter for its dressing-down (the reading of the "O' to a Haggis").

Highland Mary (Mary Campbell): Rabbie Burns's brief courtship with Mary (due to her early death) inspired several poems.

Sweeties: Scottish for anything that gives you tooth decay.

The Steamie: A Scottish play celebrating among other things the colourful language of a Glasgow gal. Translations are given to tourists.

Chapter One

DEREK

A hard-on is only as good as the hand that holds it

George, along with the rest of the cast, watched in awkward silence as Derek tried to capture the essence of Rod Stewart. With an improvised tap dance, he limped and stuttered . . .

"Do ya think I'm sexy . . ."

George, tight-lipped, used all his energy to suppress a militant yell involving a fair amount of swearing.

George had spent years ordering men around in the army and had retired with a strong urge to control. When asked to direct the panto players, he jumped at the chance and ran them like a regiment. George had "done" many pantos in his day; granted it was back in the army days when cars had four gears and seat belts were optional, but he knew his stuff and a lousy act when he saw it.

Derek stuttered, *"Come on . . . su-su-sugar let me know . . ."*

"Derek," said George through clenched teeth, "I thought we agreed to give the tap-dancing a miss this year."

Derek was about to say "the kids love it" when his plum round body overbalanced, taking the stage curtains with him on the way down.

❄

Charlie fumbled into bed. Francis, his wife, didn't move.

"You'll never guess," said Charlie.

Francis mumbled into her pillow.

Charlie looked at her back. Was she awake? He took a gamble and began to tell her about Derek's Rod Stewart.

Francis rolled over and pushed the blanket back, exposing Charlie's leg to the cold. She rose from the bed and, with a grunt, swung her legs over the side.

Charlie watched his wife stumble into the wardrobe, mutter something medical, and then hobble to the bathroom.

Charlie pulled out his notebook and wrote: *scrap Rod Stewart...*

Francis came back from the bathroom with a glass of water.

A nipple peeked through one of the many holes in her "Frankie Says Relax" T-shirt. In the half-light of his lamp, Charlie stopped to admire.

He watched her bare legs move under the covers. He loved her legs. Over the years her lean figure had become almost androgynous, except for her legs. Watching her bare legs slip into sling-back sandals was one of the highlights of the summer.

Charlie slid his hand across to her thigh; Francis pushed his hand away and rolled over with a small snort. He looked back at his page; the inspiration had gone and so had his hard-on.

Charlie met Francis twenty years ago. She had bought her first hairdressing salon and was celebrating with a few vodkas and "The Rivers of Babylon" on the jukebox. It was Charlie's first day as a barman.

Charlie made eye contact with a slim woman with dark eyelashes. She smiled at him and his tray of vodka cocktails crashed to the floor. Her slender legs didn't move an inch as he mopped up the spillage by her feet; instead her dress inched higher. He looked up, caught a flash of suspenders, and dropped the tray again. Francis picked up the glass with her toe and slid it effortlessly onto his tray.

Francis was a woman who knew what she wanted. She seduced

Charlie and he didn't know what hit him. Two sets of twins and four salons later, Francis had turned from a flexible-toed seductress to a volatile, single-minded pain in the arse with an ego the size of the Himalayas and a determination that crushed whatever lay in her path.

Francis, like George, was used to getting her own way.

Chapter Two

CHARLIE

Jazz is the Marmite of music, love it or hate it

*T*he next day, Charlie sat in front of his laptop feeling "inspired," which according to the postman was one of the many joys of celibacy . . .

His study, or spare room as Francis liked to call it, was covered in pictures and Post-its. Playing in the background was the Smiths, Charlie's "band of the month"—recommended by the same postman, who had, after a few, described the Smiths as "melancholic," "poetic," and "perfect for a man and his *one hand*."

Charlie stuck a picture of a crayon-drawn Red Riding Hood on top of a "has been" Post-it.

Charlie joined the writers' group when the twins left. Charlie was trying his hand at short stories, while George fancied himself a playwright and bored the group with long-winded monologues about the war years.

Charlie had managed to write a short love story about an overbearing woman who loved jazz and hated every man including Santa Clause and an ol' fella who hated jazz and thought spending time with women was as much fun as filling in a tax return.

Louis Armstrong, a camper van, and Santa Clause in a G-string.

Charlie was aiming for romance with a hint of erotica. What he got was the writers' group in stitches asking him to read it again, with emphasis on the G-string.

George's face lit up. *A writer with wit and no copyright?* He had a vision.

"I could use someone like you," he said.

Charlie gulped his tea. "Me?"

"For the panto, you could help me with the script."

"I've never seen a panto let alone written one," said Charlie with a mild sense of panic.

"You'll pick it up," said George.

"Pick it up? You make it sound a virus."

George chuckled. "See what I mean? Comedy is in your every pore . . . your sweat drips double entendre." (A few of the group pulled a face.)

"I am not sure. The twins have just left, and Francis has plans—redecorating, refurbishing, redesigning, and that's just the shed."

"Every line's a winner. You'll be perfect." George patted his arm.

"I'm not joking, she's a list longer than a vat receipt. It'll be the next millennium before I'm finished," said Charlie.

The postman, who for some reason was in the same room working on the heating, grunted, "That's women for you."

George eyed him. "Could you not do that when we are finished?"

The postman unscrewed a knob, the heater hissed; he looked up, spanner posed. "No amount of good writing will sort Derek."

George huffed.

"You need to tell him. He thinks his dame is what the panto needs."

Charlie had spent the next few weeks working on his Red Riding Hood. He collected pictures, scribbled notes, and took over the spare room—much to Francis's disgusts. Francis also had plans, none of which included Red Riding Hood or the Smiths.

Charlie was a house husband who had happily brought up two sets of twins while baking, making home brew, and failing to protect the endless supply of hens from a fox he had named the devil incarnate.

However, now that the last of the children had left for college, the house was empty. He had no one to bake for, and only a few scraggy hens to care for. Francis didn't do carbs, or for that matter anything eggy.

Charlie felt rudderless and past his sell-by date and spent most of his day waiting for the postman to come so they could swap Smiths songs and sightings of the fox, until George commandeered him. George had given him a script to read, along with videos of their previous pantos.

Charlie drained his coffee and turned up the Smiths . . .

Heaven knows I'm miserable now . . .

Francis entered with a *slam*, poured a gin, and with another *slam* shut the fridge.

Why do I smile at people I'd much rather kick in the eye?

Charlie waited for a "the Smiths, must we?" moan; when none came, he waited for the jazz to hit the sound waves.

Francis loved jazz. And, after a few gins, expressed that love . . . by humping her spidery silhouette to the beat with nothing on but an elastic band around her blond ponytail. It took Charlie years of "you must be joking" before he realised dancing nude was not a come-on.

He stared at his laptop, added a few flourishes of humor, and then erased them again.

Still no jazz . . .

Francis thumped up the stairs—humming. Charlie looked up as she stuck her head around the corner. She looked . . . happy? Charlie, confused, smiled back.

"Is that quiche I smell?" she said.

"Yes."

"Great!"

"Great?" He looked at her; Francis's idea of great was a polished floor, matching nail and toe polish, and an early finish at the salon, never food. He looked at his wife casually leaning against the bedroom door, looking perky—and she hadn't even touched her gin.

"Daisy loves quiche," she said.

"Daisy? What's she got to do with my quiche?"

"She's at a loose end," said Francis.

"Again? That woman has more loose ends than your clients."

"That's split ends," Francis said.

She downed her gin, let out a dramatic *that's better* sigh, and looked at Charlie. "Still helping those wankers in the panto?"

Francis had a distaste for the panto crowd on par with sex. According to her, they were as "musical as a cornered cat."

"Daisy has a theory," said Francis.

Charlie let out a *here we go* sigh. For the last few years, Daisy had slowly etched her way into their lives. Daisy was helping Francis revamp her salon and most of their revamp meetings were held in the spare room, and each time he asked how they were getting on they looked at each other like schoolgirls. Charlie's patience was wearing thinner than a crisp. He would have happily slept on the couch if it wasn't for the thought of Daisy walking in.

"She says there is more to George."

"What?" spluttered Charlie.

"And you should be careful."

"The guy owns a caravan park."

"He *was* in the army."

"Hardly MFI."

She looked at her empty glass. "She says it will not finish with a script."

Charlie, wondering what *it* was, was about to ask when Francis chipped in.

"You should be wary."

Charlie stopped. He thought about Derek. "Wary of what?" he muttered.

Francis didn't answer. She had disappeared downstairs; Daisy had arrived.

Chapter Three

THE PANTO PLAYERS

The best actors aren't found onstage

*D*erek was standing centre stage quoting his "all the nice boys love a Mars bar" speech. "Any port in a storm," Derek shouted in his best Rod Stewart voice.

No one noticed; inspired by last week's "budget" meeting, the panto players were busy dragging into the hall past panto scenery for revamping. Not an easy feat when the postman—who was in charge of the lighting, scenery, and anything else that required a screwdriver— was *sorting* the lights, causing flicking on a par with a power cut.

The rehearsals were held in the Community Hall, a run-down building with windows that refused to open but rattled as each car passed, a kitchen with cupboard spaces on par with a caravan, and a floor more lethal than black ice on tarmac.

The postman skidded his ladder across the floor with an "excuse me," "pardon," "whoops mind."

Deloris, poised over her sketchbook, motioned Derek to carry on. She was designing his costume and wanted Derek to move about the stage to get a feel for what would work.

"Go on," she muttered.

The light flickered off, then back on. "Apologies," shouted the postman.

"My name is P-p-p . . . posy Nancy, and I often feel quite d-d . . . dancy . . ."

"Is he aware that he actually stutters?" Deloris muttered to Charlie.

Charlie, along with the rest of the cast, watched in an awkward silence as Derek limped a spin, finishing with his back to the audience and a wiggle of his hips.

"A little of what you fancy does you good . . ."

George, with his director's jacket dramatically slung across his shoulder, was directing the influx of scenery with the flourish of an Italian traffic cop. He stopped mid *keep moving* gesture, glanced at the stage, and caught Derek breaking into a shoe shuffle.

Derek stopped.

"Poosie? What the hell is a Poosie?" yelled George.

The hall plunged into darkness . . .

Bump; crash.

Shit!

That'll be the lamp broken.

"I have been thinking we'll call the dame P-p-p-p . . . poosie Nancy," said Derek.

"Pussies? What the hell are you on about? And what the frig has happened to the lights?" shouted George.

"Apologies," shouted the postman.

The spotlight flashed onto Derek; he squinted. "Not pussies—P-p-p . . . poosie Nancy . . ."

"Speak up, man!" shouted George.

"That's Robbie Burns's lover that is," said the postman from the top of a ladder, mid screw. "Which is also the name of a pub, and for my mind rather a quirky pun."

"Quirky? Pun? What are you, a critic?"

"The whole world is a critic," muttered a voice in the corner.

"Aye right," muttered another.

"And," said Derek, "P-p-p-p . . . poosie Nancy could have a friend that never appears onstage, called Highland Mary . . ."

"What?" roared George.

"Or was she called Highland Fling?" muttered Derek.

"Let me get this straight: you're naming a man dressed as a woman after a pub?" said George. "Mid fling?"

"It's better than Rod Stewart," said the postman.

"Ridiculous—what man is going to get up onstage and answer to Poosie?" snapped George.

"Well, me," said Derek.

George bounded onto the stage two steps at a time and cleared his throat. "Enough with the poosies."

A few chuckled.

"We are here for a meeting."

"I'm just about to start my speech," muttered Derek.

"Thank you, Derek."

"It's new."

"Another time, Derek."

"And my designs," huffed Deloris. "They don't come out of thin air you know, I need something to work with."

Derek nodded.

George sucked in his potbelly. "We are here to discuss the script." He motioned to Charlie. Charlie walked onto the stage, peered into the dark, and waved with an embarrassed smile.

"Meet our new writer," said George.

The room fell silent; a few shuffled uncomfortably.

"No offence, Charlie," said a voice from the back.

"Er, none taken."

"But what experience has Charlie had of writing a script?"

"George is the main writer," said Charlie.

"George," said another, "was a sergeant."

"Major," said George.

"And as you'll see," said Charlie, passing around his notes, "there are a few humorous bits."

"You'll need it," chipped in the postman. "The last panto died on its arse."

"We can thank others for that," said George with a nod in Derek's direction.

"The last time a script was created 'from scratch' it emptied the hall quicker than a fire alarm," huffed Derek. "Not that many came. I mean what child wants to see *Cinderella's Dirty Dozen*?"

A few chuckled.

"A bit of war never hurt anyone," shouted George.

"A ten-minute rant about the trenches isn't funny," said Derek, "even when the actor is in a dress."

"He has a point," muttered Deloris.

"We need a proper script," muttered a voice from the back. "Something funny, not some half-baked rambling from the likes of you two . . . no offence, Charlie."

"None taken," muttered Charlie. He stared into the dark as the light flicked on. Five members of the cast stood clutching an extraordinary long Dick Whittington swinging from an even larger beanstalk.

He smiled at the blank faces.

"Why can't we just use a proper script?" said someone.

"Something amusing," said another.

"Charlie can be funny, can't you?" said George. "And who better to write a panto than a lover of jazz?"

"That's my wife," muttered Charlie. "I'm more a Smiths man."

"Who?" said Deloris.

"The Smiths," said the postman.

"Oh?" said Deloris.

She looked at Charlie and made a mental note to look up the Smiths when she returned home.

Charlie spent the next morning battling the nettles around the entrance of the shed. When he finally entered, two hens charged past him. Charlie skidded, lost his balance, and grabbed hold of the closest thing to hand—a rake—which in turn knocked over a stack of tins, along with the shelf that held the said tins. The shelf and tins crashed to the floor on top of a load of empty boxes.

Francis, who was sure he could hear laughing, shouted, "Have a good trip!"

Charlie scrambled to his feet muttering unmentionables as his head scraped against the brick wall, taking some green sticky stuff along with it.

He swore. This was not how he wanted to spend his Saturday morning, let alone the whole day.

In the end, he spent the whole weekend.

Charlie took the redundant exercise bike to the skip, along with a set of dumbbells and a deflated inflatable something covered in mould. He scrubbed the gas heater clean (in between shooing the hens), bought a new gas cylinder for the heater, and then fired it up on full and watched the only window in the shed slowly fog up.

A hen fluttered by the door and stuck its head through the rusty cat flap. He tossed the remains of a biscuit at her; she clucked as Charlie sighed.

How could he create in a shed with a peculiar smell that even a dozen scented trees could not get rid of?

The hen tentatively stepped through the cat flap. He tossed another biscuit at it . . .

He was just beginning to enjoy himself, getting into his stride as a writer—expanding his horizons, as he liked to put it. He was even looking forward to the next meeting despite the whole Derek *thing*. Then he came home to find his computer and notes sitting at the top of the stairs and his study looking like an Indian temple. Francis had told Charlie that Daisy—the "vegan" who was known by many to have the coordination of a blind eighty-year-old with Parkinson's—was moving into the "spare room."

"But that's my . . . room," said Charlie. "My study, how could you just go through everything like that?"

Charlie argued, put up a fight, but when Francis poured her third gin, he knew it was over and he should be at least grateful for Daisy. She *had* stopped Francis from throwing his notes into the fire and insisted they be kept for Charlie to sort.

He had been pushed out of his spare room by a vegan who looked more like a weightlifter than a lover of tofu. And his wife seemed happier than he could ever remember.

"Daisy has nowhere to go," she said. "Besides, you can use the shed."

"It was good enough for Roald Dahl," said Daisy, sending Francis into hysterics.

Daisy sodding Daisy. She made Francis not only smile but giggle like a schoolgirl. The only time Charlie managed that was falling over a couple of hens into an ancient oil patch. It wasn't always like that; years ago Francis couldn't get enough of him.

Later that evening Francis stood in the kitchen as Charlie picked up his laptop at the top of the stairs.

"You know Daisy has a theory," she shouted.

"So I've heard," muttered Charlie.

He tugged at the extension lead, rolled it up, and placed it on top of his laptop along with his notes.

"How long?" he shouted.

"What?"

Charlie humphed down the stairs. "Is she staying?"

"Err, well, that's the thing, we have left it open to see how things pan out."

"Pan out? What does that mean?"

"She said you'd say that."

He placed his laptop on the work surface. "And what else did she say?"

"That there is more to you than a fine quiche. And I should be wary."

"Of what," snapped Charlie, "my shortcrust?"

"No, that you're much smarter than you seem," said Francis.

Chapter Four

DELORIS

A past is often better to have than virtue

*D*eloris was a short, round woman with a past that involved a lot of men. Years ago, Deloris had been a woman of great cleavage and colour; a "looker." And there were very few locals who in their youth had not spent a memorable night with her.

George never knew the old Deloris. The Deloris he knew was the sort of woman who was surprised by nothing, had a deep ex-smoker's voice, and laughed at pretty much anything.

Everyone talked about Deloris except for George; he just liked being with her. She was easy to talk to, mull over things with, which they did every morning when they walked on the green.

George was an early riser and Deloris had Len, a dog to walk. Len was a dog well past his sell-by date and well past the hour-long march that Deloris favoured. His idea of heaven was to be by a fire with a bowl of chum and a naked toe nearby to lick. He even had a soft spot for George's toes, along with George's fire.

Len trotted in front of the couple as they took their early-morning march, George wrapped in a trench coat looking like something out of an old black-and-white detective film and Deloris staring ahead clutching her first coffee of the day.

Sometimes she could do without the march, and often wondered about handing George the lead and telling him to head off on his own. Especially during the panto season; there was only so much panto talk a woman could take with her first coffee of the day.

The truth was she tired of the same old talk, the same old faces, and going to bed with just Len at her feet. She hungered for something better, not a man old enough to be her father.

George however was full to bursting and, with no warming up "how are you" chat, burst into a panto tirade as Deloris stepped out of her door. And was still going as they marched onto the green.

Deloris, prepared with a double espresso, took a *here we go* sip.

"I want that man stopped in his tracks," George said to Deloris.

"What do you mean stopped?"

"You know, off the scene—silenced."

Deloris stopped. "Silenced?"

"Yes; somewhere else, anywhere but on that damn stage ruining my production. That man could empty a hall in one song."

Deloris breathed a sigh of relief. George was a hard man to fathom.

She watched George toss a stick into the wind with venom. Len looked at him with a *must I?* expression.

"Go on, there's a biscuit at the end," he muttered. He looked at Deloris with a pained expression. "I called him slapstick."

"Hmm. I heard."

"*He* took it as a compliment."

"Derek took slapstick as a compliment?"

"'I do my best to keep the punters happy,' he said. Now he thinks he's Charlie Chaplin . . . in pink."

Deloris sniggered.

"It's not funny, nothing I say affects that lad. I reckon he's short of a few fuses. I mean, I don't even know what he's talking about half the time, he calls his dame accessible."

"Oh, that."

"To the masses."

"He is a funny one."

George turned to Deloris with a fierce look. "There is nothing funny about ruining a production. I want Charlie to create a dame with no singing, no dancing, and in the end . . ." George took a sharp intake of breath. "No Derek."

"We're not talking anything illegal, are we? Because if we are, you can just take your panto and . . . stuff it . . ."

" . . . and you're to help persuade him."

"Persuade him to do what?"

The postman whooshed by on his bike. He skidded to a stop. Len yelped, Deloris laughed, while George jumped . . .

"Jesus man, don't do that, give a man a heart attack."

The postman slid off his bike. "Mission impossible, ol' man."

"What?"

"Getting rid of Derek?"

"I wasn't exactly talking of getting rid of but more a writing out; killing off in the first scene, act, line even . . ."

"You've got to think of the mother," said the postman.

"That ol' bat," muttered George, who had never met the woman but assumed that she must be an old bat having given birth to such a moron as Derek.

"She's the reason he's in the panto in the first place."

"He has a point," muttered Deloris.

Derek's mother was the chairperson on the panto committee, the hall committee, and the musical society; she controlled the funds, the musicians, and the hall. Some would say she was a bit of a control freak on par with George.

"She could close the whole thing if she wanted to," said the postman.

George let out an *I give up* sigh.

"Or worse, take over—get involved."

"What? My panto? Never. I'd rather eat cabbage for a week and plug my arse," said George.

Len appeared with a small stick in his mouth and an expectant *biscuit?* look. George propelled an extra-large stick across the horizon; Len's tail drooped.

"No one takes over my goddamn panto. Especially an idiot who still lives with his mother, or for that matter the idiot's mother."

George stared at Len trailing back with his stick dragging through the grass.

"She a tarter so I've heard, takes no prisoners," said the postman. "Getting rid of foot fungus would be easier than getting rid of your so-called dame."

Deloris stared ahead. She saw endless mornings of rantings, mountains of phone calls—six months at least of George bending her ear with his obsessions with Derek. She had to do something.

"There is always the costume," she muttered.

"What?"

"Remember the wedding dress?"

George's face lit up. "Yes, we can immobilise the bastard—mute him, then flood the stage with dancers—he'll be as invisible as his talent."

The postman, with a *you've taken that too far* whistle, jumped on his bike. "Poor Derek," he muttered, "have you no shame?"

"Well at least that would stop the idiot from tap-dancing," shouted George, then looked about to see that no one had heard.

Charlie had no idea about George's rewrites.

He was trying to get used to writing for a limping stuttering dame in a run-down poky shed while losing his wife to Daisy and her vegan ways. His life was heading downhill faster than a lead balloon on said hill.

His home had been turned into a shrine to womanhood with a bathroom full of oestrogen potions and two women giggling over things he didn't understand.

He was no longer needed to cook, his quiche obsolete; in fact, his kitchen was now out of bounds. Daisy ran the kitchen and shouted at him when the tofu-and-whatever-nut surprise was ready. Each mouthful was as difficult to swallow as his pride.

Daisy was a terrible cook.

One hen took a mouthful and never recovered; she was found the next day, legs pointing to the sky, beak gaping, eyes glazed. The others didn't even sniff at the leftovers let alone peck. Even the devil incarnate fox refused the food, and he ate anything. He poked about Daisy's nut loaf like it was a live snake about to pounce, yelped, and left.

Charlie retreated into the shed with bacon rolls, grieving hens, and his laptop, and he would have happily slept there if it wasn't for the hens.

Chapter Five

SANTA CLAUS AND HIS G-STRING

Even the elderly have dreams

"*A*re you wanting a custard cream?" said the postman with a sympathetic smile. He, like the rest of the cast, knew about "the vegan."

Charlie shook his head. It was his fourth rehearsal and things were not going smoothly. He was sitting in the Community Hall watching the postman pass around biscuits and feeling anything but amicable.

His karma (to quote the f—ing "vegan") was buggered, and a custard cream was the last thing on his mind.

Daisy had been on his laptop all afternoon; the "I'll just be five minutes" had turned into five hours. And Charlie had spent his hours writing notes in the shed, scraping up unwanted leftovers from the hens' dish, shooing hens from the shed, and then rewriting his notes now covered in hen shit. And Francis wasn't any help, ignoring his "is there nothing of mine sacred, does she want my balls too" protest. She had told Daisy to take as long as she liked; apparently, he had "plenty to do."

Charlie looked down at his stained, scribbled notes. He felt naked without his laptop, it was his lifeline.

Deloris arrived and took a seat beside Charlie. He nodded a small smile; she beamed back . . .

She had heard stories about his wife and wondered about a woman who befriended a known lesbian when she had Charlie to wake up to.

Charlie was nothing like the men Deloris had "been with." He wasn't striking but more *nerdy* with glasses and a full head of hair. A bonus at her time of life—most of the men she knew had hair that hadn't required a comb in years. And he was patient, not like her exes, who raged at everything from queues to television ads. Nothing bothered him, and she wondered what would.

Not that she was looking or anything. It's just that, well . . . it had been a long time.

She was just about to say something "chatty" when Derek called him over. Charlie stood up, and Deloris took in his slim hips as he casually moved to the stage.

Derek, looking agitated, pulled Charlie aside.

Deloris looked at Charlie's notebook and came across his Santa's G-string story. She began to read. It was as funny as she had heard.

"George says he's got a costume big enough for my bum, and a wig just right for my fat head," Derek whispered to Charlie.

"He said that?"

"Well, not exactly." Derek gestured to the back. "Red Riding Hood said he said that."

"George wasn't talking about your bum," muttered the postman.

Charlie looked at the postman, clutching a biscuit between his teeth while painting over last year's *this way* sign with *wolf's hangout don't go there*.

Did he ever did do anything other than fix things? thought Charlie.

"Then he said that Deloris will come over and take my measurements as long as there's no funny business."

Deloris, who had the hearing of an elephant, looked up from her second Santa read. "He said what?"

"Takes a brave man to face Deloris and her dressing pins," laughed the postman.

Deloris threw him a look.

"I'm not needing no fitting," muttered Derek. "I can make my own costume."

Deloris looked from Derek to Charlie. They were the same size.

She smiled. *Fitting a costume on Charlie would be fun, and Derek would never see it until it was too late.*

"I could bring a few dresses in for you," said Deloris. "See what you think."

Derek smiled an OK.

Now all's she had to do was convince that delicious writer to be her model.

Charlie stood at the front gate of his house. He could see the light was on in the spare room where Francis and Daisy were. "Business planning" as Francis called it.

The next-door neighbour's cat wrapped itself around Charlie's legs. He stroked her, then with a deep sigh headed into the kitchen.

The house was strangely silent. A queer feeling hit the pit of Charlie's stomach. As he entered the kitchen, the smell of burning hit him; he wondered what Daisy had been trying to cook . . . .

His scanned the surfaces; the kitchen was tidy—nothing. Then in the corner he saw it, his precious purple Mac . . .

It was no longer purple.

"There's been an accident," said Francis, walking into the kitchen. She pushed a dram in his direction. "Daisy spilt her soup."

"What?"

"She thought that the best way to get lentils out of a computer was with bleach."

"BLEACH!"

"Don't think she realised it was flammable . . . suppose anything is when it's plugged in."

Charlie stared at his computer, sitting black and buckled in the corner, with a burning feeling in his stomach making its way to his throat.

"She was on the phone straightaway . . ."

Charlie speechlessly moved the lid of the laptop. It squeaked and fell off.

"Tesco's got a sale on at the moment," said Francis. "And you'll have backed up, so . . ."

Charlie, holding the lid in his hand, looked at his wife casually leaning against the kitchen door with a disinterested look any thirteen-year-old would be proud of.

"Everyone backs up," she muttered.

Charlie, tight-lipped, shook his head. Anger rooted him to the spot as it burned in his chest.

Daisy walked in with two coffee cups, placed them on the shelf, and missed.

"I'll buy you a new one," she stuttered. "Tesco's got a sale on."

Charlie stared at his wife. His heart felt like it was pumping out of his chest.

"All my work," he said.

"It's only a panto," said Francis.

Charlie glared at his wife's blank face with rage—she didn't even care. He felt so angry he decided to get out of the house.

Francis watched his back as he walked out of the kitchen then poured herself vodka. Charlie's cooling off never took long, she told herself, and she was sure Tesco was into purple, or at least pink.

Deloris poured herself a whisky and pulled the wedding dress from her costume cupboard . . . with a bit of tweaking, she could make it even worse.

She sighed. For six months she'd had (thanks to a cousin with a slightly warped sense of humour) a vibrator sitting in her cupboard. She pulled it out and looked at it. It was big and made more noise than a washing machine on full spin . . .

She thought about Charlie's story. Laughter always made her feel sexy . . .

Santa jumped into the camper van and stretched out his hand. "You coming, love?"

Mary Christmas stared at his shirt as it fell open. A few beads of sweat meandered between the grey hairs. It had been a long time since she had seen his nipple.

Mary took his hand and decided to live a little.

And so did Deloris.

Deloris gave in to the moment, revolving around her bed in a state of hot, sweaty, quivering pleasure with more orgasms than she could remember, including her teenage years when she had put it about a bit.

The next day, Deloris got up to walk Len. She looked in the mirror and for the first time noticed the faint down on her upper lip. Without thinking she wiped it off, then pulled out a lipstick.

Chapter Six

THE HANGOVER

When it comes to toes, a dog's tongue is preferable to a cat's

The same morning, a stabbing pain in Charlie's neck woke him up. He opened his eyes to see a clear blue sky as a cool breeze whistled across his body. His clothes were damp and his feet were bare. He rubbed his head and the smell of dog shit hit him. He wiped his hand on the grass as the Smiths filled his thoughts . . .

> *I was happy in the haze of a drunken hour*
> *But heaven knows I am miserable now!*

The Comm . . . patchy memories . . .

Charlie had woken up in the same green where Deloris and George walked Len. And when Len spied Charlie's naked toes pointing to the sky, his heart leaped.

Charlie still thinking about the night before—now with a groan he felt something warm lick his toes, then Deloris's face came into view, followed by George's. He stared at Deloris. *Is she wearing lipstick?*

"I hear you were at the Comm last night," she said.

He looked at her as he struggled to sit up. "How do you know I was at the Comm?"

"Your car is parked out the front," said George.

"And you look like one of Len's dinners," said Deloris.

"Thanks," mumbled Charlie.

Charlie eased his toes from Len's licking, fumbled to stand up, and stared at the breeze playing havoc on the Loch.

The previous night was an embarrassing blur.

Charlie looked at his feet. "Where's my socks?"

George and Deloris looked at Charlie with a "thank God it's not me" look. They had both been there.

"You want us to walk you home?" said Deloris, finding his socks.

Charlie shook his head. "I'm not going back."

Deloris and George looked at each other. They had both been there too.

"That's just the hangover talking," muttered George, who had found the shoes.

"No, seriously, enough is enough, it's the car or bust."

"You're still drunk," said Deloris.

"Perhaps, but sleeping in the car is a way better option than going home. I still want to kill her."

George and Deloris didn't say anything; instead they helped Charlie to George's caravan park. It was a few minutes' walk from the green and had what many considered the best view of Loch Fyne and the garbage that washed up on the shore.

Charlie had never felt such anger before, let alone stomped it out. He raged in the car for what seemed ages, then, realising that Francis and Daisy could see him, drove off and made for the main street. He had nowhere to go apart from his car and the shed. Maybe he could find something warm to take back to the shed.

He passed the Comm, a small pub on the shore front well known for its late-night sessions. He turned around the roundabout, passed it again, and saw a backpacker posed at the entrance with a cigarette.

The backpacker waved him down. He had a pleasant face, a friendly smile, and the look of a man who liked to listen.

"Got a light?" he shouted with an Australian accent. Charlie pulled a lighter from the glove box and went over.

Next thing he knew he was puffing on a spliff.

Charlie, whose only memory of dope was a night in a strange kitchen eating anything he could lay a slab of cheese on, didn't argue. And after two smokes he felt lighter, with his love for the Smiths soaring to heights of enlightenment.

"Never heard of 'em, mate," said the backpacker.

Charlie sang a few bars. "*Hang the DJ. Hang the DJ. Hang the DJ. Hang the DJ . . .*" He skipped a few soft shoe-shuffles.

"Nup, never heard of 'em . . ."

"*Hang the DJ. Hang the DJ. Hang the DJ. Hang the DJ . . .*"

"Yeah, all right," muttered the backpacker.

Charlie offered to sing more.

The backpacker, with an *I'd rather have my nipples clamped* look, took Charlie inside and offered him a drink.

The Comm was small and old-fashioned with green walls and a sticky floor. It was empty apart from Jock and Frank the barman robustly swirling a tea towel around the inside of a glass.

"We close at ten," he muttered.

Jock sat at the corner of the bar with a view of the entrance, the toilets, and the pool table. After a certain amount of drink, Jock was known to pull out his spoons and play to any music, especially on a Friday night.

Frank the barman dreamed of the day he could sell up and spend a Friday without Jock and his bloody spoons.

Friday nights were busy: folk came in straight from work, forgot about their dinner, and stayed on for the "live music." Friday nights were for hen nights and work dos, for getting rat-arsed and pulling and, for those who didn't pull . . . picking a fight with those who did.

However, it was Monday night. And Jock had planned on an early finish.

Charlie pulled up a stool by Jock.

"You heard of the Smiths?" said the backpacker.

"Is that 'no crisps'?" said Jock.

"It's the name of a band," said Charlie.

Jock pulled out his spoons. "They're playing?" Jock looked about the empty bar. "Tonight?"

Charlie laughed. The dope had hit him, and by the time he had finished his drink, he was on a comical rant about his wife, his laptop, and soup.

"What you need," said Jock, pointing a spoon at Charlie, "is a good shag."

"Where in the name of Argyll is he gonna get that," said Frank, "the co-op?"

Charlie and the backpacker burst into hysterics. "Buy one get one free?" said the backpacker.

Charlie nearly wet himself. "Pulling? Me? My wife would rather spend an hour in a dentist's chair than five minutes with me."

The backpacker, shovelling handfuls of crisps into his mouth, sprayed, "You got a full head of hair . . . I'd shag you." He coughed. "If I were a woman."

"Me too," said Jock and then immediately regretted it.

Charlie was staring into the flames of George's fire, pondering the night before.

"The last thing I remember," said Charlie, "was throwing a dart and trying to stop my body from following." He looked up. "Never play darts with someone who doesn't speak English."

"You said he was Australian," said Deloris.

"Exactly," muttered Charlie. He sighed. "What sort of idiot drinks soup over a computer?"

Deloris said nothing.

"She used bleach. Who uses bleach on a computer?"

"Aye, well that's a vegan for you," said George, walking in with a plate of bacon.

Deloris caught his eye. They had heard many things about Francis and Daisy.

"Even my mother knows you don't use bleach. And the only thing she uses the computer for is bingo," said Charlie, glumly stroking Len.

The laptop was the least of his worries; sooner or later he would have to either crawl home or find somewhere to stay. He stared at his bacon roll, then with his hand over his mouth made for the toilet.

"Nothing worse than a hangover when your life is shit," muttered George.

Deloris nodded.

Chapter Seven

THE CARAVAN

Not everything free is worth having

George, a man who gave away nothing but the occasional hearty slap, offered Charlie a caravan. Charlie, ignoring the "you scratch my back and I scratch yours" comment, jumped at the chance.

George didn't mention that the "free" caravan was the worst in the park, with one window blocked by a hedge and the other looking out onto the laundry block.

George was a complete tight-arse.

George had been left the caravan park, and thanks to a few financial mistakes and a couple of ex-wives, it was all he had. He had never lived in a small town and not counted on the locals who, within three days of his arrival, had him down as a gambler, a womaniser, then—thanks to a set of pink pyjamas—a gay ex-escort.

Deloris told him not to mind, that after a few years he would be accepted. That was ten years ago, and he was still waiting.

The next few days, Charlie stewed like he never stewed before.

In a seventies caravan the size of a Wendy house, Charlie paced.

He thought of all he had given up: his career as a barman, his dreams of becoming more than a barman. He had cleaned and cooked, listened and supported. Now there was someone new, younger, and with a vagina; someone who claimed to make tofu tasty, who according to Francis massaged like a dream. And he was supposed to stay, take it on the chin, spend his time in the shed while they played business meeting in a bedroom?

Who did they think he was?

Twenty years of being amicable built up inside him; he padded about the caravan writing cryptic dialogue and abusive emails. Deloris, clutching pink taffeta, popped her head in, saw his silent rage, and gave it a miss. The postman gingerly knocked on the caravan, heard said cryptic dialogue, and headed for George.

"He needs someone who's been through the same thing," said the postman, "and who can take charge."

George, a man born to take charge, knew what to do.

Chapter Eight

THE LEAVING

Parting of hair is easier than the parting of one's cheeks

harlie listened to George and ventured back home. As he drove up the drive, the first he saw was his Mac sitting by the bin, looking as dejected as last night's Indian. Charlie took a deep breath and, dodging the wind chimes that now swung from the doorway, walked in.

Francis looked up from her mobile. "Here he is," she said to the twins, "you want a word?" She handed the phone to Charlie.

Charlie, ignoring his wife, silently zigzagged his way through the co-op bags into the lounge and picked up his collection of "Wilt" books and Smiths CDs.

He then headed for his room.

"He's busy," said Francis. She listened to his footsteps upstairs.

Charlie had always dealt with the twins and their problems, Charlie had always kept the house a home and the car on the road. And it was Charlie who listened to Francis late at night after she had more than a few.

Francis just assumed he would always be there no matter what. After all, she had provided for him, supported his hobbies—he should be grateful.

She watched Charlie walk down the stairs. He had three bags.

"Where are you going?" she said with her hand over the phone.

Charlie headed for the car, Francis followed. She watched Charlie place the bags in the boot and head for the shed.

"Answer me," she yelled.

Daisy took the phone from Francis. "Your mum will call back later," she said and took Francis back inside.

They stared out of the kitchen window and watched Charlie walk out of the shed with a handful of scented trees.

He kicked the bin spilling the contents on the ground, ripped scented trees into pieces tossed them onto the ground. And jumped on every bit of vegan 'thing' he could find, until he skidded on an onion skin.

"What's happening,' muttered Francis in a glazed fashion.

They watched as Charlie picked up the broken laptop, marched back into the kitchen, opened the oven placed the laptop in it and turned the oven on.

"What's he doing that for?" muttered Francis.

Daisy put her arm around Francis as Charlie without one glance at his wife walked out of kitchen and down the front drive.

"I don't understand," muttered Francis.

Charlie sat in the car and took a deep breath. George stared at his profile and watched his glasses mist a little. George didn't know Francis, but he had heard plenty.

"Feel better?" he said.

"Not really."

George started the car. "It's not good to grind your teeth."

Charlie didn't hear.

"No problem's worth a toothache." George roughly changed gear.

"Glad to be out of it," muttered Charlie. "Been thinking 'bout it for years." Charlie's face turned white. "Can you stop?"

George pulled into a lay-by.

As Charlie stepped out of the car his stomach took over . . .

"Oh, God." He spewed. He wiped his mouth.

He waited for his stomach to stop churning. He looked up at the sky; the sun was just peeking from behind a cloud. He squinted—there was no turning back.

George watched Charlie climb back into the car. Charlie tried to smile as he gingerly eased himself in. His stomach was still squeezing but there was nothing left to squeeze. Charlie took a swig of water and slipped on the only Smith's song he wanted to hear, "Please, Please, Please Let Me Get What I Want."

George told Charlie he could have the caravan for as long as he liked, along with the idea that having Deloris around fitting costumes would perk him up.

Charlie, unsure if he was perk-able, looked about the caravan. "In here?" he said.

The caravan had a peculiar smell, making him regret his attack on the scented trees.

George was about to suggest a little bleach, then stopped . . . "Open a few windows," he muttered. "Deloris won't mind."

Chapter Nine

THE WAX JOB

A quick pull is sometimes best

*D*aisy was in Francis's salon behind the counter, wondering if geranium and basil would make a good mix for a calming massage, when Deloris walked in.

"I am looking for a new look," she said.

Daisy smiled. "You've come to the right place."

Helping Deloris would take her mind off things; Francis was proving hard to live with. She had taken on the role of a wounded, abandoned wife with relish and Daisy spent most of her time consoling her. In truth, Daisy was confused; she had never seen Francis show the slightest affection or warmth toward Charlie. And now she was making out like she couldn't live without him, and nothing Daisy said made any difference.

Daisy looked at Deloris's square face; she could make that face work, and with the right colour, no one would notice the beginnings of a double chin but rather her delicious eyes. In the right light they were almost green.

"I have just the thing for you; it'll take years off you," she said.

Ignoring the "years off you" comment, Deloris followed Daisy into her treatment room. Daisy looked at Deloris's smooth olive skin and suggested some waxing.

Deloris didn't argue and stripped down as Daisy turned on the Native American CD "to awaken the Mother Earth" in her and then began to massage Deloris's legs.

"Just relax," she said, "and in no time we'll have you as smooth as Bruce Willis's head."

Daisy worked down Deloris's firm legs. As Deloris drifted into another place . . . a green field, grass waving in the wind . . .

Deloris hears the sound of a horse, and through the haze is Charlie on a horse. He stretches out his hand and pulls Deloris up . . .

"Everything okay?" said Daisy, warming her wax.

She wraps her arm around Charlie; he is wearing a ladies' corset and suspenders. She begins to undo the lace . . . .

Deloris felt something warm on her legs.

Charlie, with a tilt of his pelvis, smiles.

Rip.

"Ow!"

Rip.

"Ow!"

"You okay?"

Deloris stared at the ceiling as Daisy left the room. It had been a long time since she had her legs done.

She thought about the pleasant roll of Charlie's bum, and his clean hands. Deloris had been brought up with farming men who had hard, calloused hands that had been about more orifices than she cared to think about; they were hands that looked like tools and best kept in pockets.

Deloris pictured Charlie's slime frame and wondered how flexible he was, then wondered if perhaps it had been too long between men?

Daisy entered the room with more wax.

"Next we'll do your bikini line."

The next day Deloris turned up at the caravan park, walking a little uncomfortably but feeling polished; her legs were, for the first time in years, on show with strappy sandals and slim skirt. And her eyes were highlighted in green; she felt a bit on show and a little uncomfortable as people looked more than once.

Charlie opened the door, inhaled Daisy's patchouli mixture, and was taken back to the days when a rampant Francis had him out the back of the hotel by the beer barrels.

Chapter Ten

THE ALBATROSS

One man's dress is another man's frock

After years of wondering what it would be like to wake up without his wife, Charlie finally knew. There was no great elation, no celebrations, just an empty, rudderless feeling that wouldn't go away, except when Deloris came around.

Deloris was standing in his caravan, taking up the hem of the dame's petticoat. Charlie passed her a tea, milky with sugar, just how she liked it. He watched her negotiate the mug while clutching a pin between her teeth. She slipped a strand of red hair behind her ear and began to giggle about the caravan. "Could it be any smaller?"

The pin didn't move an inch.

Charlie was glad of her visits; they took his mind off things, stopped his thoughts circling. Thoughts that kept him awake at night. What was he going to do for money? Would he live in this matchbox of a caravan forever?

He turned as Deloris continued to pin the hem. She smelt nice.

Deloris sculled the remains of her tea, smacked her lips, and eyed Charlie.

"I need you to try something else," she said in a deep voice. "Don't worry, no pins required."

He knew she was lying.

Deloris teetered out to her car in her sandals and staggered back with a large costume bag.

Charlie eased the zip down as pink in all its shades oozed out like glittering lava. It was a ballgown with ridiculous amounts of ruffles, feathers, and taffeta, and it weighed a ton. He held it up to the light as more pink cascaded to the floor. Charlie sighed . . . it was a dress that required a full strip.

"This and me in the bathroom . . . together?" he said.

"Go on, give it a go," smiled Deloris, "you know you want to."

Charlie watched Deloris slide off her sandals and sip her coffee. She was nothing like his ex; Francis's idea of laughter was a quiet snort over the morning *Herald*. Deloris's laughter was the loud kind that filled a café, woke sleeping babies, and made any joke funny. And today she looked . . . different, colourful, easy on the eye.

Charlie, clutching mountains of taffeta, stepped into his bathroom as the trail dragged behind him. He sat on the toilet and yanked at the trail and after several attempts pulled it in, stretched across, and shut the door.

The bathroom was so small you had to sit on the toilet to clean the sink; even Charlie's weedy frame seemed to overwhelm the space. He looked at the floor covered in pink taffeta. Where could he put his feet?

He pushed a small space on the floor, stood tippy-toed, leant his knees against the toilet pan, and with a grunt eased down his trousers.

He crashed against the shower door, swung into the shower, and crashed against the soap dish.

"Bugger," snapped Charlie.

"You OK in there?" said Deloris.

Charlie, spitting imperial leather from his lips, sighed. *What's another bruise?*

Deloris waited.

Charlie pulled the underskirt over his head and with a squeeze and a twist wrapped the corset around his waist, knocked his elbow, and rubbed it.

"Bollocks!"

"How are you getting on?" said Deloris.

"Pardon?" grunted Charlie.

"I said, how's it all going?"

"I got one leg in and the other out and a pile of taffeta is caught around the S-bend—how do you think?" He tugged.

Deloris let out a loud cackle. "That's great," she said, "now all you need is this."

A hand appeared from the doorway with something frilly and very Barbie Doll pink.

Charlie held it up against him. "More pink?" he muttered.

"What's wrong with pink?" said Deloris.

"Pink is not easily worn," said Charlie.

"Pink is universal."

"Universal?"

"Yes. So what do you think, will it do the trick?"

Charlie looked at himself in the mirror. "This," he said, "is a mountain, an explosion; you'll have the audience seasick, they'll be gone before the dame even opens his mouth."

"Well, it's better than George's suggestion—red."

"Red could work."

"But it's not as funny," said Deloris.

"Perhaps you could tone down the ruffles . . . *rip* . . . and the feathers . . ." Charlie spat a couple from his mouth.

"George wanted feathers, something gay, flamboyant, and camouflage-y," she said.

"Oh," said Charlie, "I see. Well, I guess he knows what he's doing."

Deloris took the pins out of her mouth. "You reckon?"

"Well, so he says."

Charlie staggered out of the bathroom pulling at the material to follow. "This is worse than that wedding dress you made."

"So glad it works." She smiled.

"Works," said Charlie, "the dame will be lucky if he can make it out of the dressing room."

"That's the idea," said Deloris. "Stop him and his fancy ideas about dancing on the stage. Immobilise the poor guy—taffeta is his latest tactic."

Deloris turned Charlie around.

Poor bastard, thought Charlie.

"In pink," muttered Charlie.

Deloris stood back to admire, pulled a ruffle from the floor, and pinned it against Charlie's hip.

Since Charlie's great escape, there had been talk of Francis and Daisy. Deloris looked at his kind face, a man of such unexplored depth. *He is quite delicious—what a waste,* she thought, *that he should be alone.*

Charlie winced.

"If only I had the wig with me," she muttered, "I could take a photo."

"Wig? What sort of wig? Don't tell me pink?"

Deloris let out a loud laugh.

As Deloris packed away her equipment, the postman appeared.

"Thanks, Deloris," said Charlie as she left with a cryptic smile.

Charlie watched her walk away.

"What's she on?" muttered the postman.

"I don't know but she smells nice," said Charlie.

That night Charlie poured a whisky and stared at the dress. It was suspended like a dead albatross from his window, blocking his view of the shower block.

Derek was going to have a meltdown.

Charlie slept with the dress/albatross blocking the moonlight. He even dreamt about the dress . . .

Francis was in it, circling about him on a catwalk handling the dress like it was made of tissue paper while he was strapped to the catwalk unable to move, stark, bollock-ing, naked. There were stilettos, suspenders, a whip, and an audience . . .

Then—*thank God for George*—he woke in a sweat to George shouting outside his window.

George, with a wench in one hand and coffee in the other, was on his way to mend a leak in the shower block when he caught sight of Charlie's window.

"Pink? What's that Deloris is playing at?" he shouted.

He knocked on Charlie's door, then without waiting for a "come in" marched into the caravan.

"I said red."

Charlie eased himself up onto his elbow and yawned.

"She said pink was funnier and, I think, universal."

"Exactly," said George.

Confused, Charlie rustled about for something to cover himself.

"Pink," said George, "is funny."

"That's what Deloris says."

"And expected for a dame."

"That is also what she said."

"Pink is the last thing for Derek. Pink is taking too much of a chance. I want him to take one look at that dress and run . . . a mile at least."

Charlie watched George make coffee as he ranted on about Derek's inability to please an audience. "He needs to go, or this panto is doomed."

"Bit dramatic . . ."

He handed Charlie a coffee. "We're up against his mother, you know."

"What's his mother to do with pink?"

George, rummaging for biscuits, continued. "His mother wants him to stay and Derek"—George slurped his coffee—"is under her thumb. He'll do anything to please her. And pink makes it just that bit easier."

Charlie was beginning to feel sorry for Derek. He sipped his coffee as the sun beamed through the window, catching the fluorescent pink sequins. Charlie squinted as George stopped, looked at the dress, then fingered the hem.

"Although," he muttered, "it truly is a godawful dress. Even worse than that abortion of a wedding dress. It might"—he slurped his coffee again—"just work."

Chapter Eleven

THE DAME, THE PETTICOAT, AND A WHEELBARROW

It takes one man to push a wheelbarrow but many can fill it

*C*harlie felt sorry for Derek. Granted he wasn't funny, but then who was in the panto? Every joke Charlie wrote, George scored out. Charlie looked up at the pink albatross blocking the morning sun and pulled his laptop onto the bed; he still had some ideas.

For years, Charlie had lived with little inspiration. Francis had criticised it out of him. In fact, inspiration when living with Francis was as easy to get as a suntan in Scotland. Francis drank gin like tea and had a habit of shutting doors and flicking on kettles with an "it's your fault I'm miserable" slam. Even Picasso would have struggled to create living with her.

He stared at his laptop, added a few flourishes of humour, and then erased them again, his train of thought quickly evaporating as he heard Deloris thump up the caravan steps. She stuck her head around the corner of the door.

For the second time that morning he rummaged around for something to cover himself.

"Just passed Himself up to his armpits in shit. I told him it's pink or he can stuff his costumes up his arse. I'm not doing another one."

Charlie stared at his laptop.

"And I said you'd agreed!"

"What?" said Charlie.

Deloris laughed. "Got you going."

Charlie looked up at Deloris casually leaning against the kitchen door. Her round curves, the complete opposite of Francis's spidery silhouette. She looked deliciously happy.

Deloris smiled at him. "What's up?"

"George has quashed every decent joke," said Charlie. He looked at her feebly. "I'm running dry. And poor Derek's going to be standing onstage like a lemon," he sighed. "Still I think George's come around to your pink." He sighed. "Poor Derek."

"Knew he would. Always does. Remember the wedding dress," she said in her deep voice.

He watched as she removed the costume for more *tweaking*. She slid the costume into its plastic cover and began attempting to squash the trail into the bottom; a ruffle flopped out.

"Any more costumes?" he asked casually.

"Not sure what George has in mind," she said, pushing the ruffle back in; another flopped out. "Guess we'll know at the next rehearsal."

Charlie wondered if it was true about her and George—all that walking and coffee together. Pity, he thought; he liked having her around and she smelt so good.

Derek was sitting in the Community Hall watching the postman set up the special effects.

"Are you wanting a fruit slice or custard cream?" said Little Red Riding Hood to Derek with a sympathetic smile.

Little Red Riding Hood, a miniature woman of four foot five who looked like she lived on black coffee, had had her fair share of taunting. She was a single mother with two teenagers that were never out of the police station. She had faced stony faces at the school gate, curt parent-teacher's meetings, and hurtful articles in the local paper. She felt for Derek. He had yet to see the dress and she had—no one would want to be seen in that thing.

Derek shook his head. He was fed up to the pit of his bowels and a custard cream was the last thing on his mind. It was his fourth rehearsal and in that time Mr. Arsehole George had squashed every decent stage name he had come up with, along with any joke—good or bad. And his mother was on his back about standing up. *Easy for her to say.*

He muttered something about his script being "cut *yet* again."

No one answered.

George stood at the back of the hall dressed in his special director's jacket with his megaphone on full. He was hard to see in the dark, but the cast knew he was there. George was noisy man, even his breathing was loud.

"Your dress is in the dressing room, we are all waiting," bellowed George.

With an *it could be worse* smile, Little Red Riding Hood patted Derek on his shoulder.

OK, Mr. Arsehole . . . thought Derek.

Deloris slunk into the back of the hall as Derek headed into the dressing room. It was the first costume she had made that made her feel ashamed.

She slid beside Charlie.

"Has he seen it yet?"

"No," whispered the postman.

"Custard cream?" said Little Red Riding Hood with a *you should know better* look.

Deloris shook her head.

The cast waited in silence. The postman dimmed the lights. Everyone had heard about the costume; some had even seen it hanging in the dressing room with its vast trail covering the floor. No one, however, had tried to lift it.

"When you're ready," shouted George through his megaphone.

Derek limped onto the stage, his costume swooshing across the stage floor with the six-foot train rustling behind. He made an attempt to lift the sides of the dress and staggered.

"Easy," shouted George.

Derek steadied himself against a cardboard wolf mid snarl.

"How am I to d-d-d . . . dance in this? I need a wheelbarrow for this frigging petticoat let alone this . . . so called t-t-t . . . train," said Derek with a dramatic tug.

No one spoke.

"I look like a great big p-p-p . . . pink ice cream," he said.

"Pink can be funny," muttered Deloris.

Derek's exasperation boiled. "I mean this is worse than . . . the wedding dress."

Silence.

Derek stared into the dark hall searching for George's shiny bald head.

George grimaced as Derek turned and knocked the wolf to the floor.

"The scenery," he shouted.

"Standing is impossible in this," said Derek, attempting to retrieve the wolf.

"What?"

"I can't move without knocking something over." Derek stumbled. "Let alone d-d-d-d . . . dance."

The wolf clattered to the floor.

"We don't need you to dance," shouted George.

"What?"

"We are aiming for a wider audience," George's voice echoed through the hall.

Derek shouted back, "What's that got to do with my inability to stand?"

"I said we don't need you to dance," shouted George.

"My d-d-d . . . dancing is pivotal to the whole performance."

"Pivotal is not what I would call it," shouted George.

"What?" said Derek.

"We have the 'salsa' dancers now," said George.

Derek looked at Deloris and Charlie sitting in the front. "What has salsa to do with Little Red Riding Hood?"

"That's what I said," muttered Red Riding Hood.

George shouted something about broadening their reach, which no one understood.

"This is because I criticised his storyline, isn't it," muttered Derek to Charlie . . .

The cast shuffled in silence; they knew the truth.

Chapter Twelve

THE WOLF'S TAIL

A good line without good delivery is no longer a good line

*T*he day after the rehearsal, Charlie stepped into the caravan, dumped a bag of scented trees on the table, and picked up his revised script George had left on the kitchen table. He started to count George's red corrections, gave up after the first page, and flicked the kettle on.

Charlie felt a huge need to stand up for Derek. Granted he wasn't funny, but he was willing to perform in the *albatross dress* with a stutter *and* a limp. In Charlie's book, that deserved more than a stream of abuse shouted from a megaphone; that deserved a round of applause, good music, and a great line.

George didn't see it that way.

Charlie had been in the caravan for a week, and in that time, he had tried a few *let's make Derek funny* scripts. They all ended with red corrections. Convincing George that Derek deserved better was as easy as seducing Francis, and if it wasn't for the caravan Charlie would have chucked the whole thing.

Charlie tossed the script aside with an *I give up* sigh and was in the middle of hanging a scented tree when Deloris knocked and entered.

Charlie, gesturing with the tree, smiled. "Vanilla?"

"I'm more a scented candle woman," she laughed, handing him a cappuccino.

Charlie with a quick scout of his cupboards pulled out a digestive as she produced a deluxe flapjack from her bag, broke it in two, and passed the chocolate-covered half to Charlie—his favourite.

Two hours later, Deloris was still sitting in his caravan with a wolf costume over her knees like a large furry blanket. The wolf's head was across her shoulder mid snarl with two paws either side. Deloris was working on his tail.

Charlie had written a chase scene ending in the losing of the wolf's tail; it was one of the few scenes George had not changed, mainly because he hadn't seen it.

Little Red Riding Hood's father was to play the wolf. He was not the first choice, but rather standing in for a rugby-playing maths teacher who refused to take George seriously. Although both were five foot five (in heels), the maths teacher was built like a bear while Red Riding Hood's father was more like a weasel. There was a serious amount of padding to add.

Charlie looked at Deloris as she manipulated her needle. She visited most days since he had been in the caravan, usually after her walk with George and always with a coffee.

He passed her the latest script.

Deloris eyed the red crosses and sighed.

"I see George has been busy." She smiled with her best persuasive look. "Don't worry, George knows what he is doing."

"You think?"

"I know he can be stubborn," sighed Deloris.

"Stubborn? There is stubborn and there is downright cruel. Poor Derek."

"Maybe he's right." Deloris tried another smile.

Charlie threw her a look. "That Derek is better silenced, immobilised, and hidden behind a chorus line?"

"Well yes, although I wouldn't put it like that."

Charlie flicked through his script and then tossed it in the bin. "What's the poor guy ever done?"

"Well nothing I guess, it's just that George is a perfectionist."

"I mean all's the guy wants is a few funny lines; where's the harm?" said Charlie.

"Ticket sales?" said Deloris.

"Could you not persuade George to go easy on Derek?"

"I am not a miracle worker," said Deloris. She put down the fox tail. "And I am not going to spend another six months listening to George rant. Just write what George wants"—she smiled—"or I am going to take this tail and hang myself."

"Six months of ranting?"

"George is persistent, no one persuades him. I have as much influence on him as you do."

"Frank says you've got George wrapped around your finger."

"What would Frank know?" said Deloris.

Charlie blushed.

Charlie had heard about Deloris's past mostly from the postman and Frank. And Frank, like many locals, read more into Deloris and George's early morning walks than what they were, many giving Deloris the delicious fame of turning a man from pink pyjamas and men to grey shorts and women.

"Some woman love the commanding sort," said Frank, who maintained he had *done a line* with Deloris.

"He told you about us?" sighed Deloris.

"Well, in a way."

"That man and his mouth."

"He was very complimentary," said Charlie. "He said being with you was the best years of his life."

"The best years of his life?" said Deloris. "More like a couple nights in the back of a van," she sniffed. "As memorable as fish chips." She eyed Charlie. "Some fool said George *was* gay and that I turned him; do you believe that?"

"I have seen the pink PJs," muttered Charlie, "and I have seen the way he looks at you."

"He looks at everyone that way, apart for Derek," she said.

"He's good man, bit rough around the edges but don't let that fool you," said Charlie. "You could do worse."

Deloris glared at him. Was he serious? Her and George? "That's right, I could do worse than George, I could fancy a knob like Derek."

"Bit young, isn't he?" muttered Charlie.

"Or a flapjack-loving writer." She slammed her sewing box closed, followed by an abortive attempt to force the fox into a co-op bag.

"He's just my age," she snapped.

An ear flopped out, she pushed it back in, a paw fell from a hole in the corner, she pushed it back in. The tail plopped to the floor.

"Oh, bloody hell." She grimaced with a red face.

Charlie picked it up and looked at her.

He was just about to make a "never come between a writer and a flapjack" joke when George knocked on the door, causing it to creak open. He peeked in looking pleased with himself; behind him was an old TV in a wheelbarrow.

"I'm off to the dump," he said.

Charlie looked at the wheelbarrow and an idea hit him.

Deloris looked at the wheelbarrow and wished she could shove Charlie in it.

"You've anything?" said George.

"How about half this frigging place," snapped Deloris. She stumbled out of the caravan clutching her sewing box as the wolf tumbled from the bag. Both George and Charlie looked at her, confused.

George picked up the wolf.

Charlie took the bag from Deloris. "Let me," he said.

"I'm just fine," she snapped, snatching the bag and the costume.

The two men watched as Deloris opened the car boot, shoved the costume in, slammed it shut, and jumped in the driver's seat.

"What about your coffee?" said Charlie.

Deloris started up the car and with a flushed face drove off.

"What's eating her?" muttered George.

Charlie, still confused, shrugged his shoulders.

Neither noticed a tall, dignified woman dressed like a Himalayan walker approaching.

"You the owner?" she said in a deep husky voice.

"You looking for a caravan?" said George in his best posh voice.

"I am looking for George the director."

George posed. "You have struck gold."

She pulled a mobile from her pocket and pointed at a picture of Derek in the albatross dress clutching the extra-large beanstalk.

"Are you responsible for this?"

George looked at the striking woman. "It was a team effort."

Chapter Thirteen

INSPIRATION

One woman's inspirations is another man's curse

*L*ater the same night, Deloris sat in her bed with a whisky and the Smiths playing.

Girlfriend in a coma I know it's serious . . .

She thought of George, Charlie, and that big mouth Frank. She sculled her whisky and poured another. *Don't let the bastards grind you down,* she told herself, then pulled out her vibrator.

Bye bye baby goodbye . . .

George was also in bed with a large whisky reflecting on the afternoon. In five minutes, that posh attractive woman had made mincemeat of him—in his own caravan park.

"My son has more talent in his left ear than the rest of your panto players put together," she snapped, "and he has the, how you say, legs to die for."

He drained his whisky and poured another.

Her slim figure and husky European accent had thrown him off guard. She looked nothing like her son and nothing like the old bat

George had imagined. She was a stunning woman until she opened her mouth.

Catrina (or Cat as known by her friends) threatened many things, including closure of the hall with bills a mile long and an article in the local paper that would close his "dump of a caravan park."

George twirled his glass in the light, sniffed, sipped, and pondered.

George had spent years in the army, controlling, ordering, and being obeyed. He had been taught to know your enemy and plan. Now he knew her, he could plan order and the obeying would follow. He drained his glass, turned off the light, and rolled over with a smug smile. *Piece of piss.*

That same night Charlie finished the last of the action scene with a flourish, poured a tea, and looked at his work.

Confused by Deloris's exit and inspired by George's wheelbarrow, he had spent the rest of the afternoon sorting through his boxes of childhood drawings made by the twins. Big colourful pictures of Red Riding Hood and other characters, created with the intensity of a schoolgirl after watching her first panto.

He flattened the pictures out on the kitchen table, then stuck them on his wall and began to write. Charlie came up with an action/mime scene with garden furniture characters, the wheelbarrow being the sidekick for the dame's mammoth train and a deck chair "to keep George happy" being a solider. The rich tapestry of creativity had flowed through his veins all afternoon.

He decided to call Deloris.

Deloris, with a curt "why don't you tell someone who cares," threw Charlie.

"What have I done," he muttered.

She said nothing and hung up.

The next day the postman knocked on the caravan door; he had news about the *devil incarnate* fox. It had been found sprawled across the shed entrance with a half-eaten tofu burger pinned between its teeth, and the hens were keeping a wide berth. "Francis claims its old age," said the postman.

Charlie didn't know what to say. He hated the fox and yet he felt a twinge of sadness.

The postman looked at Charlie. "The end of an era, ol' man."

The postman flicked on the kettle and looked about for a mug. The caravan was a mess with childhood drawings, scraps of pink material, and synthetic fur. "Deloris been busy?" he said, pulling a mug from under a rejected wolf's tail.

"You could say that," said Charlie.

The postman blew into the mug then rinsed it under the tap.

"I hear the dress is a real monster; miles of pink Crimplene and sequins," he said, giving the mug a robust shake.

"Taffeta," muttered Charlie.

"Same thing," said the postman, hunting for the coffee...

"Don't let Deloris hear you say that," said Charlie. "She'll explode." He watched the postman spoon coffee into his mug. "Don't know what I said, but one minute she's laughing, the next, she's slamming the wolf into the car like I've just killed it. All's I said was she could do worse than George."

The postman, choking on his coffee, looked at Charlie. "George is old enough to be her grandfather."

"Well I know, but some women like older men."

"Not Deloris, she's fed up with him. All's he does is make her dog miserable."

"Len miserable?"

"And walk so fast she ends up spilling half her coffee."

"Frank says some women like that sergeant major thing," muttered Charlie.

"I wouldn't listen to him," said the postman. "The last time Frank had a shag, Tony Blair was knee deep in mad cow disease."

The postman glared at his coffee and pulled a face. "Don't let them sewing pins fool you, that's just a ploy. The only man Deloris is inter-

ested in is you. She says there's more to you than a love of corduroy."
He paused and looked at Charlie's baggy trousers. "Which is just as
well—you have any sugar?"

Charlie pointed to the sugar.

The postman pulled a rock-hard bag from the cupboard. "She's
after you," said the postman.

Charlie threw him an *aye right* look.

The postman now grimly chipping away at the block of damp sugar
said. "She is a woman of unfulfilled passion, and you're just the man to
fill it."

"Your arse."

"This is your chance, work that Charlie charm," said the postman,
tossing the spoon into the sink and looking for a knife.

Charlie looked back at his reflection. *Charm? Where?*

The postman, giving up on the sugar, looked at Charlie. "Any
biscuits?"

Charlie, pointing to the same cupboard, told him about the wheelbarrow and Deloris's flapjack quip.

The postman sucked in his breath. "Hope you haven't blown it."

"You think I've blown it?"

"Some say an angry woman is a woman in love." He dipped his
digestive. "Personally I have my doubts." He nibbled at his biscuit,
pulled a face, and tossed it in the bin. "Known a few angry women in
my time, never led to love."

"Oh."

"Well, apart from the wife."

"I see."

"She's always angry."

"So was mine."

"Yes, but we make up." He smiled at the thought . . .

Charlie slumped. Why didn't he see it? Was he that out of practise?
He sighed. *Imagine being in a caravan with a woman like her, the rain pelting
on the roof, and her laughing, enjoying things . . . .*

The postman's face lit up. "That's what you need to do—make up."

"Seriously?"

"Of course, make-up sex is the best."

"But I haven't even kissed her."

Charlie headed to the next rehearsal, his stomach hurling like a spin drier. It was bad enough being in the dark about Deloris's change of mood, but to find she fancied him?

He passed Francis's salon on the Main Street. Daisy stared glumly from the reception desk. She didn't see Charlie drive by.

Since the scented tree incident, he had only heard from Francis once, a cryptic call late at night spurred on by a decent amount of vodka.

"The twins want to know what you are playing at," she said. "I told them you're whooping it up and nothing like a man who has just left his family."

"Whooping it up," said Charlie. "I stay in a caravan with nylon sheets and a social life a grannie would be ashamed of. Hardly whooping."

Francis, without listening, ranted on about panto wankers and the ability of a cold Scottish winter in a caravan to freeze balls, bollocks, and any other swinging appendage. Charlie, a first for him, hung up.

Charlie stopped the car and watched Francis enter and the two argue. He pondered the postman's *making up* advice. There was no making up with Francis, just a leaving-to-come-around period; attempting to make up meant tantrums and the coming around being twice as long.

Daisy said something; Charlie waited for a Francis tantrum; instead she smiled. He stared . . . Daisy laughed . . . he couldn't believe it . . . then Francis kissed Daisy on the head and switched off the lights.

Chapter Fourteen

ROBBIE BURNS

A haggis by another name still requires stuffing

*D*eloris was the first person Charlie saw when he entered the hall. She looked at him and turned away; she had taken up a seat between Little Red Riding Hood and her father and was pretending to be engrossed in the fox's tail.

The postman made a *go on* face, which Charlie ignored, standing by the sound desk which two schoolgirls sat behind. They had been there all morning arranging the sound effect equipment, which was now lined up like soldiers—according to the script. With their glockenspiel beaters poised, the girls nodded a hello. Charlie returned the hello with a smile, then headed backstage.

The postman, testing the strobe light, was caught by surprise when George bounded into the hall earlier than arranged.

George made for the stage with a purposeful march as the strobe light flicked on, turning George's march to a robotic dance.

A few of the cast chuckled as George glared at the postman.

"Oops, sorry," shouted the postman.

George squinted from the stage. "Where is Derek? He is needed for the wheelbarrow scene."

Charlie cluttered onto the stage with the wheelbarrow.

"Wheelbarrow?" shouted a husky European voice from the back.

The strobe light flashed on, illuminating Catrina at the back of the hall. She was dressed in riding jodhpurs like an old-fashioned director.

"Jesus," muttered a voice from the back. The cast had heard about the showdown at the caravan park.

George switched his megaphone on full and shouted at the postman, "What the hell you playing at?"

The strobe light continued to flash as Catrina moved to the front of the stage like something out of a horror movie.

"Bloody hell," muttered another voice from the back.

"Frig's sake, man, sort the lights out," bellowed George.

The postman flicked the strobe lights off and the main lights on as Catrina appeared in front of George, along with a faint whiff of opium.

The stunned cast silently watched as Catrina and George eyed each other.

"We meet again," she said.

"Your choice, not mine."

"Yes, but I am, how you say, here anyway, and I will not be having any of your funny business."

George snorted. "Funny business with you? I'd rather have my innards stapled."

The cast gasped.

Catrina glared at the wheelbarrow, ran her finger across the top, inspected it for dust, then looked at Charlie. "You the writer of this?"

"Yes, ma'am, it's for the dame's train."

"Charlie's idea," said George.

"I see."

She pulled the script from George and nodded to the sound desk. The girls picked up the glockenspiel beaters and began to play "You Cannae Shove Your Grannie Off a Bus."

"What's she up to now?" muttered someone.

Catrina opened to a page, then began in a monotone voice to read.

"Oh you cannae shove a teapot on a table
Not without a doily and some milk
It's important to be friendly

With your table manners many
Cause you never know
Just who you're gonna meet . . ."
She stopped. "This is funny?"

"Well, not read like a German eulogy, but when sung by the chorus, then yes," said George.

"Dressed as, how you say, deck chairs?"

"With a solider for a leader," grunted Charlie.

"And this . . . this name, Poosie Nancy?" said Catrina.

"Scrapped, ma'am," said George through his megaphone.

"And . . ." said Catrina, turning a page with an exaggerated flick. "*I am here to give you a little of what you fancy, my highland flings are the talk of the steamie.*" She looked up from the script. "What is the meaning?"

The postman, posed at the top of his ladder, laughed. "That, ma'am, is a play on a Glasgow play as well as the great Bard of Ayrshire, Rabbie Burns. Two puns for the price of one."

Catrina glared; the postman's smile dropped.

"This is no time for the fitting of lights."

"That's what I told him," said George.

The postman shuffled down, muttering about *better things to do*.

"We have the new script, with new costumes."

"New script my arse," said George.

Catrina, ignoring George, turned to Charlie. "And no wheelbarrows."

"But the wheelbarrow is funny," he said.

The cast gasped again.

"No it is not, and you will change this."

"The name is Charlie, ma'am."

Catrina eyed him. "You are the same size as Derek, no?"

"Well, I . . ."

"There is a costume in the dressing room. I want you to try this on and Deloris"—she smiled at her—"work your magic . . . please."

✳

Charlie looked in the mirror and held the sickly green onesie against his face. He was going to look like an idiot.

"Hurry up, we not got all day," shouted Catrina.

Charlie pulled the onesie on, drew up the hood, and tried to walk onstage with dignity. Not easy under the heated glare of a spotlight with every footstep echoing through a silent hall. Charlie, now alone apart from the wheelbarrow, squinted into the dark, his lone green figure the sole focus of the cast.

"Lights," shouted Catrina.

"Lights," shouted George into his megaphone.

"Deloris, please," said Catrina.

"Yes, Deloris, if you will . . ." said George.

Charlie sucked in his breath as Deloris, pins clenched between her teeth, stepped onto the stage. Her heels clipped with each step.

"Never upset a dressmaker with pins," muttered the postman. Charlie threw him a look.

Deloris pulled at the lower back.

"Bit tight . . ."

"Lower down," shouted Catrina.

"Is that necessary?" muttered George.

Deloris pulled at the crotch.

"That's my balls you're crushing," he whispered.

"Is that what that was?" she whispered back.

Charlie winced. *The postman was right—Deloris with pins could be a painful affair.*

Deloris pulled tighter around the waist and secured with a pin.

"Don't move," she muttered, "could be fatal."

Charlie, feeling hopeful, assumed she was joking.

She wasn't and pulled so tight that Charlie lost his balance and tripped into the wheelbarrow. As he tried to get out, the wheelbarrow overturned. Charlie scrabbled, the postman gave him a hand, and as Charlie stood up, the wheelbarrow clattered off the stage into the orchestra pit, taking a couple of music stands with it. The triangle followed, along with a tambourine and the drums, and as crashes and ringing vibrated through the hall, Catrina huffed.

"This production is, how you say, a shambles."

Charlie caught Deloris's eye with a *thanks for nothing* glare.

Catrina turned to George. "You ran an army? I don't think so. It seems to me your command is, how they say in this country—shit."

George lifted up his megaphone to speak and she, with a militant flip of her wrist, knocked it to the ground.

The cast gasped as Deloris, for the first time ever, dropped her pins from her mouth.

Chapter Fifteen

THE PORTABLE CHIMNEY

Wet kindling is as useful as dry lips

For a week, George mulled, stewed, and huffed. He had tried to be nice, tried to communicate, but the megaphone . . . she'd taken it too far. Action rather than talk was needed.

He called an emergency rehearsal.

George was up at the crack of dawn and headed for the hall to prepare the "wolf meets grandma" scene. He planned a chase scene, a chorus, and a real fire in one of those fancy portable chimneys—to "knock her friggin' socks off"—and was in the middle of setting the fire when the cast dribbled in with confused looks. They huddled behind Granny's Soup Kitchen, each hoping the other knew what to do.

"He wants us to chase around a fire," said the wolf.

"With this on," Red Riding Hood said, gesturing to her flowing cap. "Is that safe?" She looked at Charlie. "You're the writer, do something."

Charlie gulped. George was attacking the old scenery with an axe, and no amount of health-and-safety talk was going to dissuade him. He looked like he was killing the wood.

"Excellent kindling," shouted a red-faced George.

"Three licks from a fireball," muttered the postman.

The cast, wondering what to do next, were almost relieved when Catrina arrived early.

George, engrossed in the chopping of the toadstool, didn't see her coming.

She picked up his megaphone and shouted, "Put down the axe."

He jumped, turned, and glared at her like a madman, then the two of them began to argue—Catrina insisting that her script was "how you say . . . the tits" and George claiming her script was "anything but the tits" and did not go with his "garden theme."

"You garden theme," snapped Catrina, "is stupid."

"My garden theme is brilliant and the best thing in the panto," said George.

"Thought the garden theme was your idea," whispered the postman to Charlie.

"He can have it," muttered Charlie, "I'm not arguing."

"Desperate man," whispered a cast member.

"Little Red Riding Hood's father is not a gardener and you have no idea about gardening—just look at that dump of a caravan park," said Catrina.

"Leave my dump . . . I mean park out of this," said George.

"Your gardening theme," said Catrina, "is as stupid as your war theme."

"War is never stupid," snapped George.

Catrina shouted into the megaphone, "War doesn't exist in pantomimes."

George pulled his megaphone from Catrina. "Your arse."

Catrina called George a fathead.

"This is your chance," the postman whispered to Charlie. "Impress Deloris—Catrina's paved the way . . ."

"I would hardly call it paving," said Charlie.

The postman didn't hear. "Use your charm, disarm the woman."

Charlie coughed on his tea. "You're asking me, to use charm, on that pair?"

The cast stared at him; Deloris pulled an *as if* face.

"You want me to go out there?"

The cast nodded.

"To interrupt, mid kindling-cutting, and charm?"

"Like you would," said Deloris.

George moved on to the wooden swords lying in a heap by the grannie kitchen.

The cast gasped.

"He's attacking those swords like a butcher," said Charlie. "And you want me to interrupt . . . ?" He stared at the sea of faces. "Then what?"

"You'll know what to do," said Little Red Riding Hood.

The cast again nodded.

Charlie gulped his stewed tea. *Interrupting a man like George is never a great idea, let alone a woman like Catrina.*

"You're his best pal," said a voice from the back.

"And you're funny," said another.

"Make 'em laugh, defuse," said the postman.

Deloris tutted.

"But he's past listening," said Charlie.

"Aye well, timing was never his strong point," muttered the postman.

"And he looks mad," said Charlie.

Charlie didn't do heroics; his talent had always been his ability to knock up a decent meal for his ex, dodge any flying cups, and, up to now, get along with George—and as for Catrina, she was way out of his league.

George began to rip into a speaking clock.

"If he lights that chimney," said the postman, "it will go up like petrol. That stuff's ancient—covered in flammable paint."

Charlie eyed the postman calmly stirring sugar into his tea.

"I told him, would he listen?" said the postman with a loud slurp.

Charlie knew about anger—his ex had plenty of it, and in his experience, anger was best left to simmer undisturbed, not poke at, especially when fire was involved. He wondered about a silent retreat when a voice from the back broke the silence.

"Oh shit—she's here."

The cast turned to find Derek at the stage door clutching a co-op bag with the green onesie oozing out of it.

"You're going to speak to her?" muttered a voice from the back.

He shook his head and sighed. "She is worse than him."

"Oh, for heaven's sake, I'll go," snapped Deloris.

George's moustache twitched with anger as he finally lost it. Brandishing a broken sword, he forced Catrina to give him the megaphone.

Deloris climbed onto the stage.

"Put down the mega, George, we can all hear you."

"Yes, but you're not listening."

"Just put down the megaphone and we can all go home," shouted the postman.

"This megaphone is mine," he said.

Charlie for the first time noticed the lighter attached to the megaphone. It swung loosely from the handle, like a keyring.

"Jesus," he muttered.

"Now, let's just all calm down," said Deloris, taking the megaphone from George.

Charlie sighed with relief.

"He started it," said Catrina, grabbing the megaphone from Deloris.

"She did," said George. "I just wanted to show the scene in all its glory."

He made a snatch for the megaphone; Catrina pulled it away.

"Jesus," muttered Charlie.

"A chase scene does not need a fire," said Catrina.

"You're not helping," said Deloris.

"It's pivotal," said George.

"Like the mower in your park," said Catrina.

"Mention my park once more."

Catrina glared at him. "That is no park, that is a dump."

George made a dive for his megaphone; it flew into the air and hit Deloris.

Deloris saw a flash of light, nothing more.

Chapter Sixteen

GRANNY'S SOUP KITCHEN

One man's lighter is another man's match

eorge pulled the lighter off the megaphone and the hall emptied in minutes—except for Charlie. Deloris, dazed, was sprawled out on the floor and George was flicking his lighter trying to get it to work.

Charlie, shouting, "Moustaches are flammable," bounded across the orchestra pit and grabbed George.

George swore, worming himself loose.

Charlie dived onto George and made a grab for the lighter. The lighter fell to the floor, they both dived; Charlie almost had it, then George kicked it across the stage, inches from Deloris.

"Deloris," yelled Charlie.

She didn't move. Charlie ran to her and made it before George did. He lifted her, dropped her; she came to and stumbled to her feet.

Charlie threw the lighter at her; she grabbed it.

"Run," he said, heroically lifting her over the orchestra pit.

He turned to see George pull another lighter from his pocket.

Charlie watched Deloris's back disappear out the door and sighed. *Why me?*

"Stop," he shouted, "your facial hair."

George, bent over the portable chimney, didn't hear and lit the fire.

"For Christ's sake," Charlie muttered, then raced back onto the stage as flames engulfed the portable chimney. George, with his back to the flames, pulled out a highly inflammable Dick Whittington.

"Not Dick," shouted Charlie.

George snapped Dick in half just as the flames jumped from the chimney to Granny's Soup Kitchen backdrop.

The scenery, being an old set, was also painted with flammable paint and lit up within seconds.

Charlie pulled the decapitated Dick from George's clutches, knocked him over, and rolled a now-stunned George into the orchestra pit. George clattered onto a music stand, broke three ribs, and then, landing on his dodgy hip, cracked it as well.

A spark landed on his jacket and Charlie tossed a mat of fake grass over him. Then he picked up the tea urn and tossed it at Granny's Soup Kitchen, which was now a wall of flames, followed by the milk and a pot of jam. Then he grabbed his script and like a *Mission: Impossible* Tom Cruise dived into the orchestra pit, landing beside George.

George looked up to see Granny's Soup Kitchen collapse over his chimney.

"I've lost more scenery that way," he muttered.

The cast watched as George wheeled past them on a stretcher, his face black, his coat in tatters, and his arm outstretched.

"Deloris," he shouted.

Flames licked though the gaps of the windows as the fire siren could be heard approaching.

George looked into Charlie's eyes. "Look after the park," he said, "and you can keep the garden furniture."

A fireman ran past. "There'll be no furniture left in that place."

Charlie nodded with compassion as they placed an oxygen mask back onto George's face; he, wincing in pain, pulled it down. "Deloris," he shouted.

Deloris rolled her eyes. "I am here."

He grabbed her hand. "My megaphone?"

"Didn't make it," she said.

"There's plenty more," said the ambulance man.

"Don't tell him that," said Deloris.

"It's been with me at every panto."

Deloris slipped the mask back on as George clutched her hand with a "don't leave me" plea.

"Not so tight with the hand," she muttered as she followed with a look of someone about to have their tooth removed.

"Mad bastard," muttered the postman.

"Too much pressure . . ." said the wolf.

Derek looked at his mother with relief. "Well, I guess there'll be no panto now."

Catrina, staring into the now-blazing hall, hugged her son. "There will always be a panto, son." She nodded at a fireman heading in with a hose. "Because in this sad world sometimes a man dressed as a woman is all we have."

The hall was burnt to a shell, which many saw as a blessing. And the insurance, thanks to Catrina's abusive phone calls, agreed to pick up the bill for not only a new hall but a kitchen the size of a marquee.

George, however, had no idea. Instead he languished in hospital relying on the janitor, Charlie and Deloris for information and none of them had the heart to tell him.

The day after the fire, Deloris visited George in the hospital. Armed with his pink pyjamas and shaving kit, she took a deep breath and walked into the ward.

George was delirious. Apparently, he didn't react well to pain and required the sort of painkillers used on a horse.

"Thank God you are here," muttered the nurse. "He's been talking about a Derek."

"Oh."

"Stealing his megaphones."

"He has more than one?"

George caught sight of Deloris and held out his hand. "Thank God you're here," he gripped her hand. "Where would I be without you?"

Deloris pulled her hand away; the nurse with a stiff face noticed. "He'll need looking after when he gets home," she sniffed, adjusting his blanket.

"I am no nurse," muttered Deloris.

George looked up at Deloris. "How's my Len?"

Deloris thought about Len lazing in front of the fire after their leisurely stroll.

"And my Deloris?"

"I'm no one's Deloris," said Deloris, throwing a look at the nurse. "We just walked the dog together, we are not a couple."

"It was always more than a walk," he muttered to himself.

She sighed. "I mean look at him, he's old enough to be my father."

"Everything is in good working order," waffled George.

"Working order—as if I want to see that."

The old boy in the next bed looked from the nurse to Deloris. "I'm in good working order too, but the missus . . ." He shook his head. "No interest."

Nurse mouthed "dementia" at Deloris.

"Things just need a reminder—bit of coxing." George smiled to himself.

"Aye, me too, mister."

The nurse laughed as Deloris's frustration boiled. She placed his pyjamas into a drawer, along with his shaving kit, and slammed the drawer shut.

"George, the only coxing you're going to get from me is a kick up the arse."

The ol' fella began to laugh, as Deloris looked down at George snoring like a hibernating bear.

"Do you think he got the message?" she said to the nurse.

Chapter Seventeen

THE ADMINISTRATOR

One man's bully is another's footstool

*C*atrina worked in the hospital as an administrator and regularly
intimidated the staff with an *I'm busy* scowl, a curt "not now,"
or worse, a "that is not what I am paid for" snap.

Every morning at eight she passed the ward to the office with a
coffee from the canteen. Without a smile or a nod, she'd walk into her
office and slam the door. The staff rarely bothered her; in fact, many
wondered what she did. Consultants tentatively left taped letters for
her to type, with "In your own time—much appreciated" attached.
People phoned to complain and hung up apologising, and workmen
were quickly put in their place when they approached her with a bill
higher than their quote. Catrina had the ability to cut their price in
half. In fact, so bad was her reputation that no local workman would
work for her.

The hospital regretted the day it took on Catrina and her too-
good-to-be-true CV.

As she walked past George, she caught a glimpse of him asleep
with his face screwed up in pain, occasionally muttering "Mind the
beanstalk" . . .

She stopped and sipped her coffee, catching the eye of the nurse.
The nurse quickly looked away. Catrina walked on. For the first time in

a long time she felt a stab of something; George's face of pain took her by surprise.

Derek had left school to work in the same hospital as his mother. He worked alongside the janitor, learning the trade of said janitor, while reminding him that his fly (which seemed to have a life of its own) was undone.

Derek struggled to make friends, mostly because his mother scared them off. Now, at twenty-two, he dreamed of a life without his mother, a day she would meet someone nice and stop talking about his father.

Derek's mother always saw her son onstage like his father. Derek was the image of his father, and she knew once he got the taste of laughter, he too would turn into the man she loved and missed. A man she met in the army, an entertainer in a woman's dress.

"You are like him," she used to say. "Made for the stage."

Derek was sick of hearing about a father he didn't remember. He was sick of his stupid photos in the hall, the kitchen, and the bathroom.

Did he have a limp and a stutter? Did he get laughed at?

Charlie had tried to help and talked of a script that would make him a star. Derek didn't have the heart to tell him he didn't want to be a star, let alone have his face on the panto players' Facebook page.

Now that his mother had taken over, things were even worse.

Catrina had organised for the rehearsals to continue in the school, and worse, for a photo shoot of him in the green onesie also at the school. The school was a place of painful memories for Derek and no matter how many times he told his mother Catrina ignored him giving instead her "I know best, face your demons" lecture. Soon he would be on posters everywhere, including the staff canteen, dressed in that f—ing onesie.

He sighed. Facebook was bad enough, but his face in the post office, the GP's, the bus stop?

For the first time ever, Derek wondered about running away from home.

Two weeks after the fire, Derek woke up determined to either make a run for it or do something. He could not live in a place littered with pictures of him in a green onesie.

He looked out his window and saw Sheena his next-door neighbour shoo a cat away with a bowl of water; the wind blew most of it back in her face and she swore. She was an ancient woman who spent her time staring out the window complaining no one visited her, despite the bucketloads of carers. She had a decent whisky collection, a full vocabulary of unmentionable words, and the nibble ability to parade around the room avoiding a cat hell bent on being fed. She was what some would call a character.

Derek had a way with Sheena, just as he had a way with the elderly in the hospital. He helped her with her garden, mainly clearing up her dog's mess and, in the end to avoid the mess-clearing, walking the dog. Not that the dog needed it. She was a miniature Cavalier King Charles spaniel called Pandora who circled the garden uselessly barking at anything, including Sheena's many unnamed cats.

Derek watched Pandora's circling and Sheena's swearing; she looked up and shouted him down. Pandora it seems had eaten something that upset her stomach. Derek, armed with plastic gloves, plastic bags, and a spade, headed over. He looked about the garden and picked up a couple of specimens while Sheena talked about the hall fire.

"Heard that knob is still in hospital," she said.

Derek emptied his spade into a bag, breathing through his mouth.

"Why don't you get rid of him?"

"We have, now it's Mother."

"Oh, you poor bastard." She looked up again. "Why don't you get rid of her?"

He looked at her. "If only."

"If only? What do you mean?"

"Well, she's the boss."

Sheena, shooing a cat with the corner of her dressing gown, stopped. "All groups have a constitution, it's a matter of democracy."

"Democracy?"

"Yes, we Scots invented it."

❄

Derek grabbed Pandora and her lead, then headed for the green.
Deloris would be walking the green and he knew she would jump at
the idea.

When Derek saw Deloris he let Pandora off the lead, and soon the
dogs were sniffing like old pals. Deloris smiled and waved him over;
Derek didn't think twice.

"You'll be pleased to know the dress is in storage," said Deloris
with a laugh.

"If only the onesie was as well," said Derek.

"That thing is only fit for a bonfire," said Deloris. She sighed.
"Actually, a lot of the cast are not happy."

"Mother?"

"Well, yes."

"Let's mutiny," Derek blurted out.

"We're not on a ship," said Deloris with a surprised smile.

"No, but Mother treats the panto like an army—mutiny is the only
way. And . . ." He paused. "There is the constitution."

Pandora threw herself at Len, he rolled over, Deloris laughed.
"Constitution?"

"Yes, and Charlie is up for it," he lied. Derek hadn't seen Charlie
since the fire.

Deloris's face lit up.

She looked at Derek as wind ruffled his bum fluff and almost kissed
him. Instead she said, "Sounds like fun."

Chapter Eighteen

DICK WHITTINGTON AND HIS BEANSTALK

Art is only as good as its lighting

*C*harlie was always on Deloris's mind. Every night as she lay in bed she went over the rescue, the tea urn, the fake grass, and the jam jar toss. She saw it all: Charlie's heroic hurling of George into the orchestra pit, followed by the look in his eyes.

She sighed . . .

Charlie was a real-life hero who had surprised everyone, who not only saved Deloris and George but emerged from the hall clutching the beheaded Dick Whittington, the postman's finest piece of art.

"It's all I could save," he muttered to the postman, dusting a few ashes.

"Appreciate it, ol' man."

Deloris wanted to thank Charlie, but before she could catch his eye Charlie was swept up by the ambulance men with a blanket and tea, while she had to follow George . . .

She hadn't seen Charlie since, she was too embarrassed. She had picked up the phone several times, almost walked to the caravan, and in the end chickened out.

What could she say? "I thought you were a knob until I saw you with the tea urn"? *Thank god for Derek.*

The cast met on the green the next day.

The wolf was not happy with the new chase scene, Little Red Riding Hood was not happy with the new-style grannie, and the salsa dancers, offended by Catrina's change in music, were threatening a walkout.

The postman looked about the group. "She wants me to do things her way. I told her my lighting is the pinnacle of the panto—"

"This panto has more pinnacles than the Ben Nevis," muttered the fox.

"—and," continued the postman, "it's my way or the highway."

A few chuckled as Deloris and Derek looked at each other. Between them they had contacted everyone; they had a plan, including the panto players' constitution, a threat, and a promise.

Deloris, like the others, wondered if Charlie would appear. Derek had left a message on his phone but had not heard from him. It was rumoured that he had fallen out with George, returned to his wife, even left the country on a second honeymoon.

Francis was seen loitering about the park.

Truth was George had given Charlie the keys to his home. He wanted to leave the hospital as soon as possible. He'd had enough of nurses straightening his sheets and Catrina's morning scowl, and Charlie was his only hope. Charlie not only didn't argue but jumped at the chance.

Soon he was busy looking after the caravan park, which thanks to witty Facebook jibes from Catrina actually had a few curious visitors.

"Could a caravan park be that bad?" wrote one visitor on Trip-Advisor.

Charlie, a man of many talents, made the most of the visitors. He cooked, mended, and took charge. Even Francis was shocked; she had visited sober and sheepish. She wanted him back. However, Charlie full of purpose saw a life without her, and wasn't for turning.

"You have Daisy now," he said. "You're not alone."

"But she doesn't know a thing about the hens," said Francis.

He looked at her. "Hens—since when did you care about the hens?"

Francis said nothing.

"You care about hens as much as you care about men."

"She says it's immoral to keep hens," muttered Francis.

"Is that why she fed them her cooking?"

Francis almost smiled.

Charlie took the hens along with his shed back to the caravan park. He began to think about buying more hens and talked to George about free-range eggs.

George, despite his facial bruising, smiled. "Great idea."

As the wind picked up, Charlie appeared; he had listened to Derek's message and like the rest he was curious. He had no idea there was a constitution for the panto players, let alone anyone gutsy enough to threaten Catrina.

The cast watched as Charlie approached with long strides. No one said anything but mutely watched as Len and Pandora raced across to meet Charlie.

Charlie bent to pat.

Deloris's heart skipped a beat.

"He wears corduroy well," she muttered to herself as the cast watched Charlie ruffle Pandora's head.

The dogs followed as Charlie approached the cast.

"Coffee?" said the postman, opening his flask.

"Flapjack?" said Deloris with a hopeful look.

Charlie caught Deloris's eye and said, "Let's go back to the caravan park."

"As long as you've got sugar that's not a cement block," muttered the postman.

"I have brown, white, and a fire," said Charlie.

Deloris let out an over-the-top laugh ending with a blush.

The cast discussed what they wanted as Charlie took notes, and Derek designed the petition, which to everyone's relief included a new dame for a new panto.

"And I know the man," said Derek, tucking into Deloris's flapjacks.

"Can't wait to meet him," said the postman.

Deloris squashed herself into the corner of the couch beside Little Red Riding Hood and the wolf. Charlie caught Deloris's eye; his breath stopped. Her eyes were delicious.

Charlie had tasted fear and survived. He had seen the explosion of a portable chimney, the collapse of Granny's Soup Kitchen, and, worst of all, looked into the eyes of George in his moments of madness.

Life had taken on a new meaning for Charlie, and it was too damn short for shyness. Charlie wanted Deloris to stay. He handed her his new *Red Riding Hood for Grown-Ups* story and smiled. "For you."

Relieved, Deloris beamed back and was soon reading writing that made her not only laugh but wonder about sex again.

"There ain't nothing wrong with tree hugging," said the woodcutter.

Red Riding Hood eyed him laying out his tools.

Her fingers ran along the cold steel of his implement.

"You need a little oil for this," she whispered.

Deloris sighed . . .

"You have such a way with not only a tea urn . . . but fairy tales." She laughed.

Charles tossed another log on the fire with a jaunty sway. "It takes but a genius to make the most of a tea urn."

The others with a "finally" look cut short the meeting and as they moved to go, Charlie touched Deloris's arm.

"Don't go, stay by the fire with me." He gestured to Len. "He looks too comfortable to move."

Deloris not only made herself comfortable but Charlie a new man, as Len spent the night by the fire, snoring through Deloris's laughter.

George woke up the next morning unaware of the meeting, the petition, or that Deloris and Charlie, along with Len and Pandora, were now bosom buddies.

He sipped his piss-weak tea and opened the local paper to the middle page, which was full of the hall fire along with praise for Catrina's foresight with insurance.

Tossing the paper aside in disgust, he caught sight of Herself passing. She looked worried, distracted; she didn't even look his way. *Something is wrong,* he thought. *Serves her right.* Then he pulled a face at his tea as the postman, Derek, and the janitor arrived by his bedside.

Chapter Nineteen

THE RISE OF DEREK

It's never too late to stand up for yourself

Catrina sat in her office. She was in a state of turmoil; what had happened to her son? Yesterday he arrived back from God knows where, refused to speak to her—spending time on his phone instead. He even went out again without saying where. This was a Derek she hadn't seen before.

She paced and wondered what her son was up to when a note slipped under her door.

Canteen tea break, don't be late—son.

She read the note several times; it was his handwriting. *Why a note?* She walked back through the corridor past George looking as defeated as his best war monologue. *Something is wrong,* she thought. *Serves him right.* She moved to the canteen, where she saw Derek looking sure of himself.

He smiled and waved.

She stopped . . . since when did he look so . . . comfortable? Then she saw the postman and the janitor and her stomach turned.

❄

Catrina had never experienced defeat before, let alone mutiny from her son. And she had no idea about constitutions, "the voice of the players," or "the power of vote," let alone the ability to fire any who did not respect said "committee."

"The constitution was set up years ago," said the janitor, "after the great panto riot."

Catrina stared blankly ahead; she had no idea he was taking the piss. And after two coffees and a Danish she was still confused, until her son bluntly told her she was sacked and there was nothing she could do about it.

She pushed her second cup away and turned to the janitor. "You are the dame now," she said. "And all this?" She gestured to his facial hair. "Makeup is enough?"

"He is perfect," said the postman.

"And George?"

"Sacked, Derek is directing."

Catrina choked on her Danish. "That is what I do."

"Exactly," said Derek, who hadn't stuttered once.

Snatching the last of her Danish, Catrina numbly left the table and headed back to her office to compose herself. The men expected yelling, temper tantrums, and threats, and what they got was a mother unable to deal with her son finally standing up to her. She was speechless.

As she walked down the corridor, she wondered about George. *Did he too feel betrayed?* Then she wondered why she wondered; annoyed at herself, she grimly bit into her Danish.

George was out of bed and using a way-too-short stick for balance. He was angry he had treated Charlie like a son and look how he replayed him—inviting those rebels back for coffee and *his* biscuits.

George's face flushed. He felt like a fool.

Catrina passed by and caught sight of him grimly thrusting his pink pyjamas into a plastic bag, setting off a ricochet of wobbles.

Guess he heard.

The ol' fella in the next bed shouted, "That's my stick."

George ignored him. He was too fired up.

"Mr. Pumpernickel, that's not your stick," shouted a nurse.

His name is Pumpernickel, thought Catrina, *poor bastard.*

George, not hearing, threw a strip of tablets into the plastic bag and missed. The ol' fella jumped out of bed and made for the tablets.

"Where did you get those?" shouted the nurse.

"Sweeties," shouted the ol' fella.

George turned; his stick skidded on the polished floor, and he righted himself, as the nurse banged on the glass. "Mr. Pumpernickel?"

George looked up, saw the nurse racing in followed by Catrina, lost his footing, and clattered to the floor, banging his jaw along the way. George cried in pain as the ol' fella grabbed his stick.

The nurse and Catrina came to his side; the nurse pressed the buzzer as George let out another yelp, pointing to his hip.

"I think you've broken something," said nurse.

And for the second time that morning Catrina felt a twinge of pity. "Poor bastard," she muttered.

The nurse looked at her and wondered if she heard right.

George woke up from the operation with a pain in his throat and agony in his hip; he couldn't move.

He looked across to see Catrina looking back at him.

"There is mutiny," he slurred.

"Your name is Pumpernickel?" said Catrina.

"So?" he said hoarsely.

"I need to spell it, for my files."

"There is more to me than a name," he said, closed his eyes, muttered "bollocks," and went back to sleep.

George spent the next two weeks sipping tea through a straw, eyeing Catrina as she passed by. They both had to put up with a janitor who claimed that Derek was doing a "fine job" and apparently was a "wiz at keeping the cast not only happy but inspired."

George found it "hard to believe" and often shouted it out to no one in particular.

Sometimes at the TV.

The ol' fella had a thing for *Murder She Wrote*; in fact it was the only thing that kept the ol' fella entertained, claiming that "Jessica Fletcher and I are like that" followed by an abortive attempt to cross his gnarled fingers. According to the nurse, his wife was the image of Jessica Fletcher.

George claimed he was desperate to go home and could not take a fifth "Hooray for Homicide" even if it did keep the ol' fella from stealing his sweets. Those in the hospital were desperate to see the back of him, including Catrina. Walking past him was putting her off her morning coffee—so she said, a little too fervently, some thought.

Every morning Catrina stomped her way through the corridor, and every morning, as George heard her heels clip across the corridor, he waited with his planned finger gesture. Soon the ol' fella was mimicking his gestures followed by a gleeful chuckle.

Catrina never flinched; in fact, she maintained eye contact like a dog standing his ground. It took her three days, two "up yours," and one "giving the finger" gesture to answer back.

"Just scratching my nose," said George.

"Yes, well it is big," she snapped with a grand Italian "up yours" gesture.

George heart skipped a beat; she had the spirit of a cougar. The cleaner, watching the unexpected flourish of Catrina's forearm, nearly choked on his chewing gum—and, with an extra-hard squeeze of his mop in the bucket, made a mental note to design his floor mopping around the George and Catrina "up yours" hand signal show.

George was a man with an empty home life. He had spent a lifetime paying for three failed marriages and a widowed mother, none of whom he understood.

He thought all women were like his mother—happy to obey. His father was a tyrant, and it was only in his mother's last years he realised being with him was, as she said, "no picnic."

"If I had my time over again," she said, "he wouldn't even be in it."

George's confusion soared. He thought she was happy. Catrina was different; she never looked happy and was as direct as a snake bite. She brought out the fire in him he thought was long buried.

The day he was told he could leave, George's mixture of emotions swirled inside him. *Who could he insult now?* Let alone expand his rude hand gestures with?

Catrina walked past clutching her morning Americano, expecting the usual barrage of insults, only to see the George's back bent over the bed, packing; a pang of disappointment stabbed her in her chest.

"Packing? Thank God for that," she said.

"Aye, and you were the last to know. So much for running things."

The janitor was by the sink unblocking a U-bend full of sweetie wrappers—care of the ol' fella. He looked up, catching the eye of the cleaner mid swirl of the floor mop.

"I run things," said Catrina, moving into the room. "This hospital would come to a standstill without me."

The cleaner's mop swirls slowed.

"In your dreams," said George. "You scare everyone—look at your son."

"My son? It was you who bullied him. Can't wait to see the back of you—you old goat."

Charlie arrived with Derek behind him. "You ready to go . . ." He stopped.

"Me, a goat—you're an old bat."

The old boy turned up the TV. "Shhh, Jessica's just about to catch the thief."

"Bat? How very dare you—glad to see the back of you and that rat moustache."

Catrina turned, attempting a spin of great panache.

"The wet floor . . ." said the cleaner.

"Mind," shouted the janitor.

"Shhh," snapped the ol' fella.

Catrina slipped backward; George caught her back, easing her into a tango-like pose.

She looked up.

He looked down . . .

Their eyes met.

The *Murder She Wrote* theme tune began . . .

"Missed the ending," muttered the old fella.

Chapter Twenty

TRIPADVISOR

To trip up is not the same as trip over

hen George arrived home, he was surprised to see campers. "It's Catrina who started it all," said Charlie. "What? How?"

Charlie showed George Catrina's comments on TripAdvisor and Facebook; scathing but funny.

"I'm no camp-and-go sort of woman, but one look at this place and I was off quicker than a kids pop-up tent. I'd rather have my innards stapled than camp in that dump."

"She stole my line," muttered George. "I'll have her." And before his bag was unpacked, before Charlie could boil the kettle, George was striding down the road to Catrina's cosy cottage by the canal.

Catrina for her part had spent the day shuffling in front of George's empty bed, only to see the ol' fella blankly staring at the TV, or worse, gesturing to the empty bed and shrugging his shoulders.

She went home and wondered, *Who is there to shout at now?* when she heard a loud bang on the door. She peeped through the keyhole and saw George's round face, red.

She smiled.

"What the frig are you wanting?" she shouted.

"You and your witchlike comments—you called my dump a park on Facebook . . ." He stopped.

"Dump a park?"

"I mean park a dump."

He made to knock on her door again as Catrina opened the door and glared.

George readjusted himself. "So what have you to say for yourself?"

"Nothing."

"Nothing?"

"Nothing."

They looked at each other.

The postman rode past, rung his bike bell; neither heard.

Derek walked up the front path. "Hi, George," he said.

George grunted.

"You coming in?" said Derek.

George and Catrina followed Derek into the kitchen. Derek whistled as he pulled bread from the cupboard. "Excuse me." He gestured to the fridge, George moved.

Derek pulled out butter, cheese, tomato, then a cucumber, followed by a prolonged look at the length. Still whistling, he began to construct a sandwich of epic portion with exaggerated care.

"Few folk at the park, huh?" Derek sliced chunks of cheese. "Not bad for this time of the year." He offered a slice to George, who shook his head. "You'll have noticed a few changes?"

"You finished?" said Catrina.

"Nearly."

"It's a sandwich," said Catrina. "How long does it take?"

Derek began the process of putting everything back in their containers, then gestured for George to move from the cupboard.

"Charlie's done a great job," Derek said.

"I know," said George.

Derek moved to the stairs and stopped. "It was Mother that started it all."

George, eyeing the curve of Catrina's neck and with thoughts of kissing, muttered, "I know."

As Derek headed up the stairs to his room, Catrina offered George a drink. "Whisky?"

George nodded, eyeing Catrina's slim legs as she moved to the whisky bottle.

"You run?" he said.

"Of course, how do you know?"

"Your legs."

"What is wrong with them?"

"They are racehorse legs."

"You being funny?"

"Very aerodynamic."

"Could you describe my legs in a less 'engineering' way?"

"Amazing."

Derek switched the TV on in his room and the theme tune for *Murder She Wrote* filtered down the stairs. George looked at Catrina and they both smiled.

Catrina poured them a drink, "Ice?"

George nodded.

She handed him the glass, their fingers touched and neither moved.

George looked up from Catrina's bed; the rain was pelting down. Catrina, eyes closed, was smiling. He felt like he was floating; never had he been taken before, and Catrina not only took him but rode him like a wild horse.

She pulled him into her bedroom and kissed him like there was no tomorrow. And for a while George wondered if there was as his heart raced like a hamster in a wheel.

"Mr. Pumpernickel," she whispered. "You rise well."

Rise well? he thought. He rose like a sixteen-year-old first thing in the morning, in fact better than he remembered.

George slept for ages and woke in the morning rising with little more than a touch for another round.

"I'm no 'shag and go' man," he whispered.

"Mr. Pumpernickel," she whispered back, "I was banking on it."

George kissed her neck.

EPILOGUE

Deloris organised a dress rehearsal for reviewers and, thanks to their reviews, the first night was a full house. George limped into the hall on opening night. He stood at the back and along with Catrina watched the audience laugh in all the right places, shout for more, and give a standing ovation. Poosie Nancy and speaking garden furniture was a total hit.

George had a lot to be grateful for; so had Catrina. A caravan park worth marching about in and someone to march, argue, and make up with.

And it was all thanks to Charlie's panto.

After the panto, Charlie walked home inspired; he was full of ideas for bigger and funnier pantos and Deloris was eager to listen. As they entered the caravan park, he burst into song . . .

"My name is Poosie Nancy, and I may have what you fancy . . ."

Deloris laughed as the neighbour's cat wrapped itself around Charlie's legs. Charlie danced a few steps about the cat in a dame-like fashion, then stroked the cat.

His new caravan was at the posh end of the park with a view and a patio. Charlie opened the door and the central heating welcomed them.

Deloris smiled.

"This is a panto-free area," he said. "Just you and me."

"Finally," laughed Deloris, "I can stop bringing around costumes for you to try on—just to see you."

"As if you would," laughed Charlie.

The End

Would you like to read more?
Novella 2 ***Panto Boy*** is out now at your favourite store...
Turn the page for a taster

PANTO BOY

Chapter One

Agnus wants a second chance on stage. Her partners want her to grow old quietly. Will their relationship survive or fizzle out like a damp sparkler?

Deirdre moved in with Agnus after her husband, a meat-and-two-veg man, had decided that he no longer wanted to be married to a woman whose idea of "meat and two veg" was a nut loaf with "green stuff."

Deirdre, a little relieved, rented a run-down shop next to Poundstretcher. She cleared the mouse droppings, painted a mandala, and started dabbling in herbs and anything organic. Deirdre's Vegan is the New Black shop was her dream, a fantasy that had kept her going for years.

"Vegetables are fun," she used to say to her husband, which usually had him choking on his sausages. He hated vegetables and would not consider eating one except when grated, camouflaged or stuffed into meat.

Vegan is the New Black was slow to pick up. In fact, Deirdre was so out of pocket she was forced to move into the back of the shop to save money. Vegetables and soya were sniffed at by most, and it was only when she splashed out a window display of her new Goddess and Beyond creams that women began to show interest.

Along with her vegan food, Deirdre made creams and potions for stretch marks, wrinkles, and achy joints. And when woman started asking for more, Deirdre, working harder, upped her production. Soon, she told herself, she'd be as busy as the chippy down the road; all's she needed was a bit of luck and a marketing plan as cheap as a packet of crisps.

It was autumn when Agnus visited the Vegan is the New Black shop. She walked in stiff-lipped and headachy. She had spent the best part of a morning arguing with her partner about the whole "principal boy thing."

Agnus had an audition for the local panto and, as usual, was "going for" the principal boy. Agnus had a strut worth watching, and she knew it; every year she pulled out her leggings, extra-high boots, and a fetching hat to do just that: strut through her audition.

The principal boy was the be-all and end-all to her. Standing onstage singing "All the Nice Girls Love A Sailor" and the like was heaven to her, she loved camp, dressing up and applause. And now at the rip old age of sixty-five she wanted one last bite of the cherry.

Her partner Lesley, however, had had enough. For years she protested; George's pantos filled her with dread. Every autumn she moaned to a blank face, deaf ears, and a parade of leggings, hats and hopeful "What do you think?" looks. Agnus fretted about her age, and over the years preparing for her audition had turned into a series of "do I look old in this" moans that pushed Lesley's patience to the limits.

Once the panto season started, Lesley hardly saw Agnus, apart from times when Agnus, anxious about her age, demanded feedback about her latest costume. Appearing with a "gorgeous or what?" pose, Agnus would stand in front of the TV, usually at a crucial moment; the punch line of a joke, the winner of *Strictly Come Dancing* or, worse of all, *Gardener's Question Time*.

Lesley lived for the day that Agnus would hang up her hat and join her on the couch. When they could plan the garden, bet on who wins *Strictly Come Dancing*, or laugh at a punchline together.

In fact, she was so desperate she organised a surprise sixty-something, birthday-come-retirement party. Lesley had high hopes that Agnus would take the hint and give up.

The panto players presented Agnus with a "have a great retirement" shield along with a year's subscription for *Saga* magazine. Lesley even took Agnus on a retirement cruise and was stunned into silence when Agnus waltzed into the kitchen sporting velvet leggings, leather boots, and a "ta-da" pose.

Lesley looked up from her bacon and exploded.

"I thought we agreed that you were to stop all this malarkey."

"Malarkey? Panto is hardly malarkey," said Agnus.

"But the cruise, the panto shield, the *Saga* magazine . . ."

Agnus sighed. "I need this."

"This?"

"Treading the boards, the standing ovations."

"No one does standing ovations in Lochgilphead."

Agnus threw her a look.

"Don't know why you frigging bother," muttered Lesley.

Agnus pouted.

"No one gives a monkey about that knob George and his productions."

"I do."

"That man's pantos have taken boredom to a whole new level. And as for that bubbling fool Derek, watching him play the dame is as painful as stepping on an upright plug."

"But I'm not . . . painful to watch," said Agnus.

"It's just a wee panto, in a wee church hall for old folks; even the schoolkids are dragged along under the promise of a free McDonald's."

"That a total exaggeration," said Agnus, "there's no McDonald's for miles."

"Just once I would like a normal winter: you, me, and *Strictly Come Dancing* on the telly."

Agnus slumped. "I hate *Strictly*."

"Why don't you take up gardening with me?"

Agnus pulled a face.

"Walking then?"

"Walking? I am a dancer, a master of the high kick."

Lesley tutted.

"Just one last dance, that's all I want."

Lesley, scraping butter onto her toast with venom, scowled.

"Is that too much to ask?" said Agnus.

Lesley muttered a "flabby around the chops" insult, squeezed her bacon into a sandwich, and headed into the garden.

Agnus, with a sigh, pulled a few faces in the mirror. Was her jaw flabby? Was she too old? She twisted to see her bum, held in her stomach, and then pulled a red-carpet pose. Maybe a better bra, a tan?

Then she remembered Deirdre's Goddess and Beyond shop display. The chemist who had smooth, tanned skin had not stopped talking about it, and she should have retired years ago . . .

***

Novella 2 **Panto Boy** is out now at your favourite store....

A NOTE FROM THE AUTHOR

I hope you enjoyed Charlie's adventures inspired by my time performing in the local pantomime. Although there was no fire I did meet some impressive characters some of who inspired the characters in this book although I am not going to tell you who.

You can find me at

www.kerrienoor.com

Like me at

facebook.com/kerrienoorwriter

twitter.com/kezzamac

instagram.com/kerrienoor

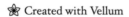

ALSO BY KERRIE NOOR

Bellydancing and Beyond Series:-

Sheryl's Last Stand Book 1

The Downfall of a Belly dancer Book 2

Four Takeaways and a Funeral Book 3

Three Angry Women and A Baby Book 4

And

Planet Hyman Series :-

Rebel Without a Clue Book 1

Rebel Without a Bra Book 2

Rebel Without A Crew Book 3

And

Diva Diaries Series:-

A Dame Called Derek Novella 1

Panto Boy Novella 2

Panto Girl Novella 3

And

A Dress For A Queen And Other Short Stories

if you loved *A Dame Called Derek*

please leave a review.

My gratitude will hold no bounds

Regards and cheers

Kerrie Noor

THANKYOU'S

Editor– the lovely Sarah Kolb-Williams
Book cover designer–The wonderful libzyyy @ 99 designs
And...
Ye ole Adrishaig Amateur Dramatic Society
We had a lot of fun

Lightning Source UK Ltd.
Milton Keynes UK
UKHW010641170322
400211UK00001B/266

9 781999 644758